Australian Folk Tales

Also by Elizabeth May Winter

Fairyland
Self Published
Printed by Community Books Australia,
P O Box 589,
Darling Heights,
Queensland
Australia 4350

Australian Folk Tales

Elizabeth May Winters

Trafford Publishing

Elizabeth May Winter

56 Magnussens Road,
Tingoora
Queensland
Australia   4608

Mail Service 1395,
Wooroolin.
Queensland
Australia   4608

Ph/Fax: (07) 41690394
e-mail: bwinter@harboursat.com.au

Order this book online at www.trafford.com
or email orders@trafford.com

Most Trafford titles are also available at major online book retailers.

Sketch and Cover design by:
Elenora Niester

Natures Transformation Drawing by:
Robyn Dower

Printed in Victoria, BC, Canada.

ISBN: 978-1-4269-2103-2

*Our mission is to efficiently provide the world's finest, most comprehensive book publishing
service, enabling every author to experience success. To find out how to publish your book, your
way, and have it available worldwide, visit us online at www.trafford.com*

Trafford rev. 11/05/2009

 www.trafford.com

North America & international
toll-free: 1 888 232 4444 (USA & Canada)
phone: 250 383 6864 ♦ fax: 812 355 4082

To Mary Currie my special pen-pal for 38 years who passed away on the 19th May 2009.

Foreword

This book is a culmination of short stories. Most of them were centered around very real animals we have here on our property in Tingoora and a neighbour's farm near by.

The Anniversary Waltz is a love story between three people: Alistair, Kathleen and her mother's ghost.

Beaky was written about my pet magpie whose mother abandoned him when he was only a few weeks old.

Bitza was a Kelpie cross cattle dog who loved children and was very faithful and loyal to the whole family.

Last Christmas I was asked by a friend of my daughter (Heidi) to write several stories for her children as Christmas presents and Bronte's Bullock became one of them. It was written about an enormous gentle Bull with giant horns. This bull is my neighbour's pet bull 'Cherokee' that follows her everywhere.

Fifteen kilometres from our property is a town Named Wondai which is an Aboriginal word meaning place of dingoes. This gave me the idea for Cry of the Wild. We often see true wild dingoes passing through our property.

Contents

F. NIESLER

Anci's Birthday Party

For the past six years Anci and her little dog Puttsy had lived with Granny Appleseed out in the country far away from the nearest town.

Granny Appleseed suggested to Anci that she may have a party for her Birthday this year. There were no other children where they were living so Granny Appleseed wondered who she could invite. This puzzled her for days. Anci said to Granny one day, "Can I invite anyone to my party?"

"Yes, Anci you may invite anyone," said Granny.

Anci remembered the fairy folk that lived in the Old Willow Tree. She wondered how she could get in touch with them. In two days it would be her seventh birthday so she had to find a way to contact them as Granny will need to know how many to cater for.

Anci sat down at Granny's desk and taking out some of her special notepaper she began writing a letter to the Little Folk of the Old Willow Tree.

Little Folk,
Old Willow Tree,
Dear Little Folk,

For your kind deeds in helping to cure me after Old Spinners bite and for bringing me home safely
I would like to invite all the Pixies, Fairies and elves to my seventh birthday party.
It begins on Friday afternoon around 2 o'clock. Follow the cobbled path until you come to the big
cream house with green trimmings.
Please reply by tomorrow.

Yours Faithfully,
Anci.

It was a lovely morning as Anci and Puttsy skipped down the cobbled path to find a letter written to Anci by the little folk. It was written on pale cream paper bark.

Anci,
The Big Cream House

Dear Anci,

The Little Folk from the old willow tree would like very much to attend your seventh birthday party.
We will bring our toadstool seats and some ant cookies, dandelion tea and some sweet nectar from the bumble bees honey trees. Our Fairy folk orchestra would love to play for you.
You can expect us all at 2pm sharp.

Thanking you for your kind invitation,
Yours Faithfully,
The Little Folk.

Anci said "Oh! How exciting, the little folk are coming to my party, Puttsy."
She read the letter out loud again to Puttsy and then said "We must go and show this to Granny."
Anci's little dog Puttsy jumped around and woofed loudly for he was just as excited as she was.

Granny read the note carefully and said to Anci, "There is much to do so we had better start after lunch. What do you think that they would like to eat Anci," asked Granny.

"We could make some fairy bread with lots of hundred's and thousands on it and some pale pink and lemon iced fairy cakes," suggested Anci.

Granny thought for a second and then said, "that sounds like a great idea."

Granny and Anci were so busy that they hardly noticed that daylight was fading into night. Granny told Anci that it was time for her to go to bed.

Granny said as she tucked Anci in, "Goodnight Anci, pleasant dreams."

Anci was too excited to go to bed but eventually she fell asleep and dreamt about Mr. Prickle's hole in the ground and The Pumpkin Twin Fairies as well as the fairy nurses and Old Spinner's web.

Next morning Anci was still very excited as she and Puttsy woke early. Granny had breakfast already on the table when Anci and Puttsy arrived. Anci did the dishes while Granny sorted out some of her finest lace table cloths and doilies. Anci gave Granny a hand to set up some small tables and place the beautiful lace table cloths on them. Just before 2 o'clock Anci and Granny laid the tables with lovely fairy bread with lots of hundred's and thousand's sprinkled all over them and beautiful fairy cakes covered with pale pink and lemon icing.

As the fairies, pixies and elves came through the pale green door in the old willow tree Granny's old Grandfather clock began chiming. It was two o'clock and the little folk had promptly arrived on time. Granny Appleseed opened the door to the house and the little folk filed in one at a time with their rather large toadstool seats. In one corner of the room the fairy orchestra set up their little instruments. They waited until all had eaten and when granny brought out Anci's birthday cake they began to play Happy Birthday.

While the fairy orchestra played. Soft sweet fairy bells tinkled and rang throughout the house. Granny gave Anci her birthday present. It was a big pink and purple girl's bike.

"Oh! Thank you Granny," Anci cried with delight.

"I thought a bike would be a great idea. You are old enough now to be able to ride it to school."

Granny handed her another present and this one was from Puttsy. Anci opened it and there was a small, beautifully coloured ball. Puttsy woofed and woofed as if he was saying to Anci come out and play. Puttsy loved to fetch balls or sticks he was happy to bring them all back.

"Not now Puttsy. Can't you see that we have guests?"

The fairies gave Anci a beautiful box full of assorted flower bulbs. There were sweet smelling yellow and orange butter cups, white daisies, yellow daffodils and yellow and orange jonquils. "If you plant them at the end of winter each year when spring comes Granny will have a lovely and colourful array of flowers growing in her gardens."

The elves had made for Anci a lovely instrument that can predict the weather. Out of an old twisted willow tree the elves had carved a little house with crooked windows and a crooked door. To tell the weather they had made Granny and Anci popping out of the little windows almost like a cuckoo clock to announce if it was going to rain or stay fine. Anci was delighted with her gift.

The pixies had brought her a beautiful china mushroom jar full of the sweetest dew drop and honey nectar from the special bumble bees trees in their enchanted forest.

The last present was delivered by the fairies to Anci from Old Spinner. He had spun her a beautiful table cloth made from the finest thin gossamer silver thread that he could make.

"Oh! How lovely," Anci cried. "This will make Granny's and my food even more special to eat. Thank you. Thank you all for the lovely presents."

Old Mr. Time had flown by so quickly and now it was time for Anci to say goodbye to her special guests from the old willow tree. Anci, Granny and Puttsy walked as far as they could down to the end of the cobbled path with the fairies, pixies and elves. As each one said goodbye they would take their rather large mushroom stools and pop through the little pale green door back into their little world. After the last one popped through Granny, Anci and Puttsy watched as the pale green door slowly disappeared.

Later when Granny tucked Anci into bed she said," Anci, it would not be wise to tell others about your party today. They might not understand. Let's keep it our secret shall we?"

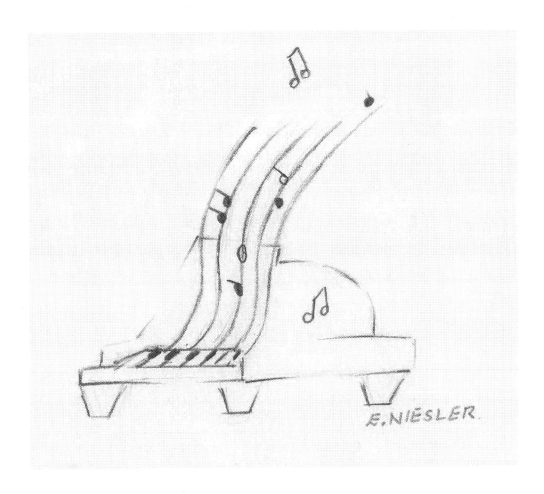

Anniversary Waltz

Alistair sat on the edge of the bed listening to the voices emulating from within the light-hearted laughter that echoed throughout the house.

He could hear someone saying, "Something old, something new, something borrowed, something blue".

It was exactly thirty years to the day when he and his true love married. He allowed his mind to wander back through time to when they first met at the annual festival. She stood out among the crowd with her smooth olive complexion, dark eyes and wavy brown hair that shone like silk in the warm sunlight. His loss came a few days after his daughter Kathleen's birth.

Just then a light tap on the door brought him back to the present as Kathleen peeped in saying, "The photographer is here."

He watched as she walked across the room in her mother's slightly altered wedding dress. She also displayed her same striking features. The photographer entered the room as she sat down in front of the large round mirror.

Putting his arms around her Alistair said lovingly "Kathleen, you look as lovely as a picture and so like your mother. If only she could see you now. She would be so proud."

She looked up at him with her dark eyes saying, "I have something new and something blue, now I need something old and borrowed."

Leaning forward Alistair opened the piano music box and as the Anniversary Waltz gently filled the air he took out the gold necklace he had given his wife on their wedding day and handed it to Kathleen saying, I'm sure your mother would want you to have this." The engraving on the locket read, "Our love is forever." Kathleen felt a lump in her throat as she asked her Dad to help her put it on. As he placed the necklace around her slender neck it fell gently on the antique lace dress. Alistair whispered: "This was my gift to your mother, now it's my gift to you. I hope it brings you only happiness and pleasure."

As the photographer took his last picture the cars arrived to take them to the church. It was a warm, sunny autumn day as Kathleen entered the Anglican Church thirty years after her mother and father had. Walking down the same aisle she could see Cameron's smiling face looking back at her.

Before God and those present, Kathleen and Cameron pledged their everlasting love. Confetti and rice filled their hair as they emerged from the vestry on their way to the reception.

Kathleen chose the music for the bridal waltz carefully as she knew that it was her father's favourite because it always reminded him of her mother. Later that evening Kathleen and Cameron danced and for the second time that day the Anniversary Waltz filled the air. After they had waltzed around the room several times Alistair tapped Cameron on the shoulder. Cameron stepped aside and Alistair in his mind had stepped back in time to finish the dance with his two most favourite people – Kathleen and her mother.

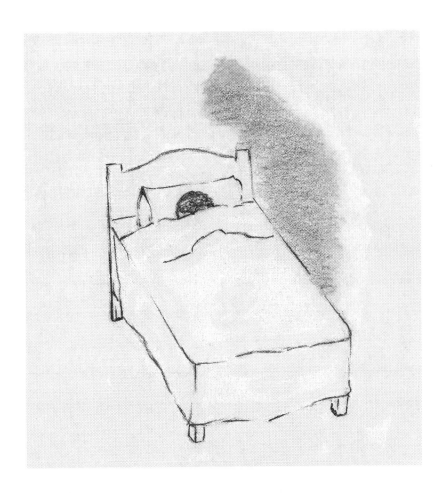

Apparition

After Tez's husband committed suicide, she and her small children were devastated. Because of debts encountered by Tez after his death she had to sell their family home. Tez packed the car and bundled her small children in and headed for a little country town. Unpacking completed Tez found it difficult to sleep in her new house. There were many new sounds for her to cope with. Somehow living in a small country town was different from living in the big city they left behind.

Tez's room was at the top of the stairway. One night Tez put the children to bed in the room at the end of the darkened hallway. When the last child had fallen asleep, Tez closed the door quietly and walked to her room.

Tez had an unusually restless night but in the wee hours of the morn she finally fell asleep. Suddenly Tez was awake and sitting upright in her bed. What had woken her? She didn't remember any loud sounds. Quickly she sprang out of bed and started running towards the children's rooms.

She screamed as she turned to face the illuminated figure coming from the darkened hallway. The door to the children's room opened and the ghostly apparition was standing there watching the children while they slept.

As Tez entered the children's room the figure had disappeared. Strange as it seems Tez was not afraid. She had convinced herself the ghostly apparition was that of her late husband making sure that they were all safe.

Beaky
(A Magical Magpie)

The waiting room seemed unusually packed but it wasn't long before Elizabeth and Bradley Simmons were called in to receive the results of Jydan's tests. They left Jydan in the corner rocking backwards and forwards with his hands clasped together, and stepped inside knowing that he would be right there when they returned. As they walked through, Dr. Sheedy greeted them with, "Hello, Elizabeth, Bradley. I wish I had better news for you. Jydan is suffering from a form of Autism." He further explained that doctors don't understand exactly why but Autism happens when part of the brain shuts down and in Jydan's case it is affecting his ability to process information in the right order for it to be of any real use to him. He continued, "As he is already five and still unable to speak except for a few noises now and again it is unlikely that he will ever learn although it does prove he is not deaf".

They left Dr. Sheedy's office now knowing that there was a reason, a condition if you like, for Jydan's problem; Autism.

That afternoon, while they were still trying to absorb this news, Bradley's transfer with the bank came through. He was allocated another position in a small Australian country town, one of the few real bush towns left. After Bradley told Elizabeth the good news he asked, "You don't seem too enthusiastic." He put his arms around her and said, "What's really bothering you?"

"Jydan is, Bradley. What if they don't accept him?" she replied.

Everything packed, they took a long last look at the place they had lived in for so long and headed for the bush.

When they arrived they were amazed at the diversity of such a small farming community and the vast range of small crops grown. Grapes were grown for the winery also a variety of corn, peanuts, wheat, sorghum and duboisia. Driving through the countryside they saw a colourful array of cows, goats and horses scattered throughout, occasionally drinking water from the muddy dams that sparkled like jewels in the sunlight.

A few weeks later when Bradley was down the paddock, he saw a baby magpie fall from the nest while its mother was trying to teach it to fly. After a few more attempts to get it to fly, the mother abandoned it. Bradley picked it up and brought it up to Elizabeth to look after.

They named the magpie "Beaky" and as the months went by and under Elizabeth's care, he had learned to fly. But, because of the fall, it could not fly properly or stand up without falling over to one side. Therefore he could never return to the wild as she had hoped. It wasn't long before Jydan became friends with Beaky, as he liked to walk around the floor and sit on the table and chairs as well as Elizabeth's shoulder and hands. Beaky had not only begun to call like a magpie but had also learned to say a few words. Elizabeth would talk to him and he would listen intently when she called Jydan or told Beaky to shut up.

One day while Jydan was sitting on the floor and Beaky was being very vocal it happened. Elizabeth couldn't believe her ears as she spun around thinking to herself, "Did I really hear what I think I did?" Jydan had told Beaky to shut up. It seemed Beaky wasn't the only one listening to Elizabeth when she spoke.

Later that evening when Bradley arrived home Elizabeth rushed out and gave him a huge hug saying thank you between kisses. Laughing with delight he asked, "Now what's all this about?"

Taking his hand she led him into the living room. "Ssh! just listen," she said. The words Elizabeth used the most were, Beaky, Jydan and shut up. Much to Bradley's surprise Jydan, although still sitting and rocking in the corner was saying as Beaky walked around in front of him, "Jyn, Beks and shup." It was a start. Bradley was astonished.

Jydan had learned to talk because of their new home and a magical magpie.

Bitza
(The Wonder Dog)

Bitza was three months old when Marina found him. He was lying on some bags of fertilizer sleeping upside-down in the back of a caged trailer at the local Saturday morning flea market. She knew immediately that he was a special dog. The sign on the cage read: For Sale, Kelpie/Cattle Cross Pups, $20 each. when Marina stopped to look, the woman asked, "Which one would you like?"

Marina replied, "The upside-down one as long as he's a male. He looks like he'll be a real character." Taking him from the cage, the woman said as she handed him over "A nice choice and yes he's a male." Marina paid the woman and took her pup home as a companion for her two-year-old son Peter.

Arriving home Marina emerged from the car with the pup in her arms.

David immediately asked, "What have you got there? What have you gone and done? Don't tell me you've bought another dog. You just can't resist can you? You can't go to the markets without buying something. By the look of his paws he'll be a big dog." After Marina told him the dogs' breed David said, "We'll call him Bitza." And in the months that followed they would come to appreciate just how special he was

Every morning Bitza would go to work in the paddocks with David. He would spend his days following the tractor up and down the rows as David ploughed the ground between the trees. For a little more excitement he would chase a hare or two, even a kangaroo or emu passing through. To see the direction that they headed in, he would jump up as high as he could while running through the long grass. He never caught the kangaroos as they were too fast for him although he did catch the occasional hare. He would stand over them with his paw pinning them to the ground as if to say, "Look at me! I'm clever! Now, what do I do with them?" Then removing his paw the hare would be off at high-speed.

At breakfast David told Marina the he and Bitza would be working in the paddock near the dam. After they left Marina got on with her chores but soon realized how quiet it was. Peter wasn't there continually asking her questions or wanting her to do something for him. Where was he? Marina called him but no reply. She ran outside in a panic frantically calling, "Peter, Peter, where are you?"

Peter had also decided to go to work with dad. He wandered from the side of the house where the road ran down to the dam and the adjoining paddocks. Busy ploughing, David hadn't noticed Peter walking along the top of the dam wall but Bitza was ever watchful. By now Marina was running down the paddock frantically looking and calling for Peter. Peter tried to turn round when he heard his mother call but slipped and tumbled down hitting his head on a rock rendering him unconscious and then he hit the water.

David stopped the tractor as he spotted Bitza taking off across the paddock towards the dam. With his ears back and his long stride this jet-black dog looked so graceful as he raced across the paddocks. Peter was floating face down in the water as Bitza reached the dam. Down the wall and into the water Bitza plunged. Grabbing Peter's shirt he pulled him to the edge where David and Marina helped pull the unconscious boy from the water. While Marina laid him on his side to revive him, David jumped in the old Landrover and headed for the house to call an ambulance.

The media reported Bitza as "The wonder dog," who saved a little boy from tragedy.

After Marina and David brought Peter home from the hospital, they all attended a ceremony for Bitza, presenting him with the highest honour, a bravery award. A huge Bone!

Blue Bonnet

Down in the fairy garden at number 56 lived a mischievous elf named Blue Bonnet. He was small for his age so his baggy pants always seemed rather large. The pixies would often laugh at him because he walked everywhere on tippy toes and wore brightly coloured mismatched clothes such as bright orange shirts with red and purple pants and a royal blue bonnet with a finely woven gossamer lime green thread trim.

Blue Bonnet would spend all day playing tricks on the pixies and all night dreaming up what new ones he could play on them next day. His favourite tricks included filling gum nuts with beetle juice and throwing them at the pixies or dropping furry caterpillars down their shirts to make them itch. Sometimes he would make the dew drops on the bluebells fall on any unsuspecting pixie as they passed by.

This made Blue Bonnet laugh and laugh although it didn't amuse the pixies and they didn't like him at all. In fact they often called out to him "Walk on your feet properly little fairy" to get back at him for all his silly little pranks. Blue Bonnet became very sad because no-one wanted to play with him anymore. The fairies noticed this and brought it to the attention of the Fairy Queen.

It was almost Christmas and the Fairy Queen had summoned Blue Bonnet because she had decided that he had caused havoc in the garden with his mischievous pranks for long enough.

Shyly Blue Bonnet visited the Fairy Queen in her chambers.

"Blue Bonnet," said the Fairy Queen, "I have a lovely surprise for you. I trust you have heard of St. Nicholas?"

"Santa Claus?" answered Blue Bonnet. Er! Yes! Of course I've heard of him. Why?" he asked.

The Fairy Queen replied, "Santa is looking for a new elf to help make toys for all the girls and boys to whom he delivers presents at Christmas time. Would you like to become one of Santa's helpers?"

"Oh, yes! I would," cried Blue Bonnet with joy.

"Then go and pack your best clothes and be back here within the hour as Santa himself will be coming to collect you. And Blue Bonnet, mind you say a proper goodbye to all your friends. You must remember you will be going to the North Pole with Santa to work; therefore, there can be no more of your mischievous pranks. Promise me!" demanded the Fairy Queen.

"I promise," replied Blue Bonnet.

Sure enough, Blue Bonnet was packed and ready and had said his goodbyes to all his friends just before Santa arrived an hour later.

Formalities out of the way the Fairy Queen entrusted Blue Bonnet into Santa's care knowing that he would be acquiring a new helper and she had restored peace to the garden at number 56. And Blue Bonnet was always on his best behaviour.

E.NIESLER

Bronte's Bullock

Bronte was sitting on a hay bale watching his pet with its huge horns gently nudging the young cow. He was daydreaming about the day his father had taken him to the rodeo. For it was there that Bronte had decided to himself what he would really like for his birthday.

At the rodeo Bronte had been taken for a ride around the grounds on the back of a camel. Afterwards as Bronte and his father weaved their way in and out of the large crowds of people, they sometimes caught a glimpse of this small grey very young sad looking bull that had been locked in a cage for hours. Being only thirteen at the time and coming from a farm where all the animals were allowed to run free Bronte turned to his father and asked, "Why is the poor thing locked up in a cage all day?" Bronte's father replied that he didn't know. Bronte, muttering, said to himself, "I wish he was mine! I'd set him free! He could roam and run all day in the paddocks with all our other cows." He shuddered at the thought of this poor little bull becoming a rodeo star.

Just then they passed a hot dog stand and as if to take Bronte's mind off the bull his father suggested that now would be a good time to have lunch. They stopped at the hot dog van but it was too crowded as were the next two. The next van sold Paddy's Hot Potatoes and Cranston Pies so that became the lunch menu.

"Oh! Look dad," shouted Bronte, "there's a tent over there where we can sit in the shade and have our lunch without being trampled."

As they ate they watched the riders attempting to ride some of the horses. Bronte turned to his dad and stated, "They don't stay on very long do they?" Seeing Bronte was engrossed in watching the bulls bucking, his dad told him to wait here and he would be back shortly and then they would be off home.

Once out of sight Bronte's father headed for Mr. Saunder's office. He knocked on the door and a loud voice yelled, "Come on in." After a little negotiation and bargaining they came to an arrangement whereby Bronte's father could take the little grey bull home. Mr. Saunders helped him load the bull onto his Ute and the tarp acted as a dual purpose. As the clouds started to build it would stop the rain and keep Bronte's surprise birthday present a secret at the same time.

A softly spoken voice brought Bronte's thoughts back to the present. "A Penny for them," she said and then asked, "I've seen that look before. Your father gets it all the time. What was so good that it has distracted you from your duties for so long?"

You know mum it must be, what, well on eleven years since dad surprised me with Cherokee, and hasn't he grown into an impressive bullock?

When I purchase my own farm I'd like to take him with me so that he can spend the rest of his days free ranging on the long luscious grasses in the paddock. You know despite his huge size he has never hurt any of the other cows. Oh! Sure with his horns he may give them a butt now and then to move them along out of his way. Cherokee gets on well with all the animals. He's a gentle giant not just to the other cows but also to the horses, donkeys, chickens, goats, geese, dogs and peacocks.

"Well," replied Bronte's mum, "your father will be some what less than a gentle giant if you don't have your chores finished before he comes home," she warned as she walked away. "Now stop your daydreaming and get on with it."

"Yes, mum," she heard him call back.

E nicalen

Cry of the Wild

On this still morning as Bucko knelt beside his wife's grave he could feel her presence and hear the leaves rustling as he began to say his final goodbyes.

"Well old thing," he said gently touching her headstone, "It's time I were off then. Never been one for lengthy tarahs. You and I built a good life together near Dingo Creek. It'll be lonely now without you."

Not game to look back, with tears in his eyes he turned and walked towards his old Landy, turned it over and headed back to the bush. Catherine and Bucko had never been separated before so it was not surprising that he spent his first night alone restless and uneasy.

He woke to the sound of Tom calling. "Bucko," as he thumped on the door. Bucko greeted him with, "What's all the shoutin' about? Billy's on, come in."

"Just thought you'd like to know the dingoes are back. A few of 'em been shot round here in the last day or two."

"Sure they're not foxes? We've not seen dingoes round here for a long time," inquired Bucko.

"Nope," said Tom. "Ain't no mistakin' a dingo, mate. Could be one wounded though. Old man Marshall's eyesight's goin' so he thinks he only injured the one he shot. It would pay to keep and eye out," suggested Tom.

They talked and after a cup of tea Tom left to spread the word to other locals.

Later that evening when Bucko was sitting on the front veranda he could see two small mysterious lights in the grass. A closer look revealed they were the yellow eyes of a young wounded dingo pup. As he gently carried the pup inside, he thought, "What would Catherine do?"

Thinking out loud he answered; "Yes, she'd look after it, but would that be wise? In the past many farmers had lost stock to these wild, beautiful, creatures, so keeping it could bring unnecessary problems."

Just then Catherine's voice broke in; "But it's a helpless puppy. You might get away with it if they thought you brought it back with you." Examining the pup he found that it had a large flesh wound. A fair amount of care, love and attention would soon put that right.

During the years that followed the loneliness he felt from the loss of his wife had been replaced. Bucko's property was not within walking distance of his neighbours so if any questions were asked, Tom would simply say; "If it helps him cope with Catherine's loss then I'm all for it."

Summer had ended and winter was fast approaching and for the first time, Bucko had sensed the restlessness in the young dingo. It was inevitable! The call of the wild was too strong. Bucko knew that he would soon lose his friend.

As the dingoes howled one cold and frosty night Bucko knew they were calling the pup. Slowly he got up to open the door and the eyes of the pup met his. No words were needed, as the dog knew he was free. Free to come and go as he pleased.

Free to return to the wild!

Deanna's Dream

Little did I realize as I awoke this morning that I would face one of the hardest and most exciting challenges of my teaching career.

Ring! Ring!

Ring! Ring!

Oh! No! It's 5:45am. Who would be calling at this hour I thought as I slowly picked up the telephone.

"Hello" I said still half asleep.

"Hello. Good morning. Is that Robyn?" said a quiet voice on the other end of the line.

"Yes, it is" I replied.

"My name is Samantha Sinclair and I am enquiring about music tuition for my daughter." She paused for a few moments and then said "You see I am having difficulty finding a tutor who will accept her as a student."

Before I could ask what the problem was she began. Other tutors have suggested to me that it is impossible to teach deaf children music. When I ask why they reply that it is important students can hear. It's a common belief that students must be able to hear to be able to play successfully." In a quiet trembling voice she asked, "Would you?" She hesitated for a moment. "Would you be willing to tutor a partly deaf child? I'll understand if you feel that it would be impossible, but Deanna will be so disappointed as her dream has always been to play in an orchestra."

I thought that if this were the case then why do we teach our students to read music?

But wait! Think a minute!

If all students can hear, then they could all play by ear and there would be no real need for music tutors.

Samantha was presenting me with an enormous challenge and one that I didn't hesitate to accept.

Samantha was a tall, slender woman with dark brown hair while Deanna, who was eight years old, was tall for her age with sandy blond hair that fell in curls.

Samantha began, "You may think that Deanna is staring at you but she is only reading your lips. If you position yourself where she can read your lips it will make all the difference."

As Deanna's chosen instrument was the piano, her first lesson began with the basic rudiments of music.

Ah! Ha! This piece will do nicely. Turning around I was perplexed to see Deanna just sitting there staring at me, and it was at this point that I realized my mistake. Until now, Deanna had been sitting at the piano and I had been standing and walking behind her, a position I often took while teaching hearing children. Then I remembered Deanna was not a hearing child. Sitting down beside her I turned her face towards me remembering her mother's comments before the lesson. Just then there was a disturbance and I turned my head in time to see my cat tearing through the music room closely followed by next door's dog, Sasha.

Smiling and shaking my head I turned towards Deanna and said, "Oh, yes! Now where were we?"

Samantha arrived for Deanna just as the lesson ended.

While waiting for Deanna to arrive for her next lesson, I began filing some old music away when I came across one that had always been a special favourite of mine. Father had brought it with him from Ireland many years before and was one that he liked to play on his violin.

"Perhaps Deanna would like this piece. Yes, I'll show it to her." Just then the doorbell ringing interrupted my thoughts. "That will be her now."

For Deanna the same place, same time, had become a regular habit now. She had begun to show great promise from the first lesson and her dream of playing in an orchestra was well on its way to becoming a reality.

I needed to speak to Samantha so asked if she had a few moments to talk with me about Deanna

"Is anything wrong." she queried.

I replied, "Deanna is doing fine and that's what I want to talk to you about. I'll be the first one to admit that when you brought Deanna to me eight years ago her dream was almost impossible considering her disability. It has become obvious that she has talent and I now believe her dream can become a reality. In a few weeks my students will play at my end of year concert so I have invited a special guest to hear Deanna play. During the weeks prior to this I would like Deanna to have a few extra lessons in preparation for Mr. Chimes' visit.

Deanna's big chance had finally arrived. Preparations had gone well and now it was up to her.

As Mr. Chimes sat in the front row enjoying the concert, Samantha and Robyn's nerves were on edge. Would he or wouldn't he?

After the concert and while Robyn presented her students with their achievement and exam awards Mr. Chimes had a long chat with Deanna.

Robyn addressed the audience. "Excuse me everyone, our special guest Mr. Chimes would like to speak."

Mr. Chimes took to the stage. "Good evening Robyn, students, ladies and gentlemen. I would like to thank Robyn and her students for a most enjoyable evening. For those who do not know, I am currently the director of the Parish Orchestra and tonight I would like to present Deanna with the honour of becoming our orchestra's new pianist."

Farmer Jack and the
Cabbage Patch Rabbits

Early one spring morning as farmer Jack was wandering through his cabbage patch he stumbled on an unusual sight. For just on the outskirts of the patch in a rather obscure place, he found growing, alongside the old twisted pink apple blossom tree, one enormous cabbage and a smaller one close by. The big one was as big as the tree.

Farmer Jack scratched his head and whispered to himself, "I wonder how they came to be growing there? I know for sure that I didn't plant them." As if to answer himself he said, "Possibly a parrot, crow, magpie or butcher bird had picked up some seeds sometime when he was planting and dropped them. Or perhaps the planting seeds may have blown here by the wind." He stood there admiring the green, lemon and lime leaves of the one gigantic cabbage and the smaller one adjoining. Then he noticed first the freshly dug dirt around each cabbage in his patch and that it was free of weeds. Also, several families of rabbits had built their homes in the cabbages.

In the gigantic cabbage they had created four separate houses. Almost at the crest of the cabbage the first home was built of small, fine brown bricks. It looked rather stately sitting above the old twisted pink apple blossom tree. The front door and landing was sheltered by an outer large cabbage leaf that curled backwards. In the front of the house were four small pale green windows that allowed the sun to filter in. Mr. and Mrs. Henry and Henrietta Hare who occupied the first home often admired the blossoms on the tree outside. Out through the top of the gigantic cabbage was the chimney to the fireplace built from the same bricks and looked like a turret from an old English castle.

Underneath the first home was the entrance to the second dwelling and the granny flat built in the side of the smaller adjacent cabbage. In the side of the smaller cabbage was another pale green window from which the rabbit's grandparents Mr. and Mrs. Edward and Florence Bunny-Hop could see the pink fungi growing on the outer walls of the cabbage leaves. The entrance to the second house where Mr. and Mrs. Elizabeth and Marcus Long-Ears lived was made of small brown bricks with a nicely carved wooden box next to the front door for the firewood. The heavy wooden front door with its pale green glass windows allowed the rabbits to see who was calling. You could walk right through to the other side and stand under the arch way leading out into the soft grass surroundings. Near the front door was a walkway made of small marble chips that separated the second house from the granny flat and a brown stone wall that stopped the water from the well coming in.

At the side of the well wall on a large brown log lay Peter Cottontail dressed in his long blue pants and long-sleeved yellow shirt dropping pebbles into the water. Nearby was the blue stone wall and the nine steps and three landings leading up to the third residence at the foot of the gigantic cabbage. It too had a large wooden door with pale green glass windows.

On the opposite side was the fourth abode where Mr. and Mrs. Toby and Angela Bunya-Twistle-Nose lived. Their doors and windows were protected by another enormous green, lemon and lime backward curling cabbage leaf. Through the pale green windows Peter and Kiara Cottontail would often be seen eating their meals in the garden on the soft green grass during the summer time.

After several hours work in the cabbage patch every morning at 10 o'clock all the residents from the different homes would gather in the garden for morning tea. Just then the door at the crest of the gigantic cabbage opened and Mr. and Mrs. Henry and Henrietta came out to greet farmer Jack. Formalities over they invited farmer Jack to sit down at the table and have morning tea. Henrietta explained the others would be along in a while after they completed their daily tasks. "And what tasks would they be?" enquired farmer Jack.

Henry replied, "Did you notice that your entire cabbage patch was weeded and the ground freshly dug around them?"

"Yes I did." answered farmer Jack.

In response Henry stated, "Because you allow us to live here in complete harmony that's the least we can do for you."

One by one Henry introduced farmer Jack to the other residents as they arrived for morning tea. Farmer Jack enjoyed his morning tea and chatting to the rabbits and on leaving he promised to come calling more often.

As he wandered back to the house on that fine spring morning he couldn't wait to tell his wife of his early morning experience with the cabbage houses, the rabbits and the service they provided him with.

Grandma's Yellow Roses

Where Grandma lived it was the middle of summer which was one of the hottest, longest and driest on record. Late in the afternoon Grandma stood in the doorway looking out over her gardens where an array of beautifully scented white roses had been planted. "Philby, is there no end to this blessed drought? Oh! Just look at my poor roses. I keep watering them but the bore water barely keeps them alive. They need rain and lots of it. Unless we get rain soon, I don't know how much longer they will last."

"Don't worry dear," Philby said patronizingly, "after all it has to rain one day, doesn't it? If it's any consolation, everyone round here is in the same boat, aren't they?" he said sarcastically.

"You're right as usual but that doesn't make it any easier, now does it?" grumbled Grandma. Just then Dee Jay piped in with, "Hey Mum! Can't you ask those little people I often see you talking to? You know, the special ones down in the gully."

"You mean that part of the farm that your mother gaily refers to as "Fern Tree Gully's Fairyland," chirped Philby laughing.

"Well it was just a suggestion," retorted Dee Jay.

"Oh! Boy! Have you really seen them then?" Philby enquired.

"Of course I haven't. I just see mum chattering away some times when she's down there, that's all."

"Oh! Dee Jay, don't mind him. He's just being a skeptic as usual. I think it's a wonderful idea. First thing tomorrow I'll write them a note and ask if I can visit. Would you like to come?'

"No thanks," he replied quickly but shyly.

Early next morning grandma sat down at her desk. She lovingly took out some of her finest paper embossed with gold edging. Then, putting pen to paper wrote to her special friends.

Your Royal Highness,
55 Mushroom Palace,
Fern Tree Gully,
Windy Hill.

Dear Queen Amberlyn,

I respectfully ask that I may visit 'Fern Tree Gully's Fairyland' for morning tea say around 11 o'clock. There is something of great importance that I wish to discuss with you. It is a problem I hope the good citizens of Fairyland may be able to help me with.
I await your reply,

I remain respectfully yours,
Grandma Winter

Grandma folded the letter carefully and popped it in a gilded envelope. Then she walked quickly and silently down to Fern Tree Gully's Fairyland. She gently dropped the letter in the opening in the big old brown and gold leafed tree that grew on the edge of the gully. Walking back slowly to her home on windy Hill Grandma wondered why only she could see Fern Tree Gully's Fairyland and its special occupants. Thinking out loud, Grandma exclaimed, "Why can't Philby and Dee Jay see them? Is it because they don't really believe that Fairyland, her royal highness the fairy queen, pixies, fairies and elves exist or do these special inhabitants choose who they present themselves to?" Grandma found this to be a perplexing question.

Arriving back at the house she had just sat down in her rocking chair on the side verandah overlooking the gully when a shy young sprightly elf appeared. He was dressed in Austrian type clothes with boots that looked too large for his tiny feet. On his head he wore a what almost looked like a babies blue bonnet. Grandma gave a polite giggle at his appearance with his very knobby knees, his big, black eyes and his very crooked nose. He clambered up the stairs rather awkwardly. Bowing slightly, he held out his hand and said, "My name is Grunch and I am one of the Fairy Queen's elf messengers."

He handed grandma a letter from his fairy queen carefully written on creamy coloured paper bark. Grandma bowed gracefully and accepted the letter.

The elf spoke quietly, "I have been instructed by the queen to escort you to the palace gardens where morning tea will be served."

The Big House,
On Windy Hill

Dear Grandma Winter,

My loyal citizens the pixies, fairies, elves and myself cordially invite you to come and take tea with us. We'd love to work together with you to find a solution to whatever your problem may be.

We await your arrival.
Her Majesty,
Queen Amberlyn.

Grandma hurried inside to find her prettiest dress and shawl to wear to the Fairy Queen's morning tea. Once downstairs, Grandma followed the young elf down the charming but secretive and magical cobbled pathway, past the rock wall where some of the edge dwellers live. The elf led Grandma over the tiny bridge that spanned the sparkling water.

The peaceful flowing brook meandered its way gently down through Fern Tree Gully and into Fairyland. Grandma stopped on the bridge to gaze around at the beauty that is seen only by a selected few. Turning to the elf, Grandma asked, "Where does the stream come from?"

"Look up," he said pointing to the hilly area of the farm. "It comes from that delightful waterfall."

Grandma looked towards the hill and saw the enchanted waterfall gently falling. The magical waterfall glistened like tiny diamonds and colourful crystal dew drops in the early morning sunlight. Just then Grandma heard the young elf say, "We must hurry as it is almost time for tea and the fairy queen does not like to be kept waiting."

They hurried through the ancient parts of Fern Tree Gully's Fairyland passing the old historical flour mill carved out of a huge twisted old tree that had stood there for several centuries and then on to the baker's house.

"His family has served and supplied food for the former queens and all of Fairyland from ancient times through to the present day. The water mill from a bygone era still pumps the water up for every day use in the baker's kitchen." explained the elf.

He led Grandma past the rows of bellflowers, buttercups and little mushroom houses where the pixies, fairies and elves sleep when the sun sets at the end of the day in Fern Tree Gully's Fairyland.

They hurried across the open grassy fields of the Fairy Queen's palace where morning tea was about to be served. Grandma Winter curtseyed to the Fairy Queen.

Pouring tea and handing it to Grandma the Fairy Queen quietly said, "I do so enjoy your friendly visits." Then she calmly asked, "Tell me your problem and I'll see if we can come up with a solution."

Grandma slowly sipped her dandelion tea then placing her cup back on the fancy saucer Grandma began to explain, "As you may have noticed we have had the longest, hottest and driest summer on record. My problem is that Philby and Dee Jay have in the past dug up the rocky soil and they have made gardens and planted an array of some of the most beautifully scented white roses. Sadly the drought is slowly killing them."

Queen Amberlyn suggested that there was an easy solution to Grandma's problem. She enquired, "I assume your plants are similar to ours Grandma Winter?" The Fairy Queen continued, "When our plants begin to wilt we simply water them. Now how much easier can that be?"

The Fairy Queen was rather pleased with her answer until Grandma's gracious reply.

"Watering is definitely the solution but because the rain hasn't come we need to conserve this valuable commodity for our use. It is vital we do this in order for us to survive so we may continue to live off the land in this harsh environment. It is unfortunate but we cannot afford to waste it on our plants regardless of how beautiful they are."

Grandma studied the Fairy Queen's face and hoped that she had not been too blunt. However, she felt that it needed to be said in order for the Queen to understand the severity of the problem.

That problem having been addressed, the ladies continued quietly chatting. Together they calmly cured all the ills of the world. Grandma rose and the Fairy Queen summonsed Grunch to lead Grandma back to her house on Windy Hill. Before leaving, Grandma curtseyed to the Fairy Queen. Queen Amberlyn remarked that she had a very pleasant morning and would discuss the problem with her subjects and hopefully find a solution. After Grandma and Grunch disappeared from sight Queen Amberlyn gave the pixies their orders. They were to invite all the residents of Fern Tree Gully's Fairyland to a meeting in the big hall. As the last of the pixies, fairies and elves straggled in and sat down, Queen Amberlyn arrived. When quiet prevailed she rose to address them. "Citizens of Fairyland, Grandma Winter has a serious problem and she has asked for our assistance in solving it. "Queen Amberlyn went to great lengths to explain the situation and offered a reward to anyone who could quickly come up with a practical and logical solution.

Grandma's dilemma was the talk of the entire village. As one of the elves was hurrying past her, the Yellow Fairy who had been down gathering water lilies stopped him and asked what all the fuss was about.

"We need to come up with a solution to Grandma Winter's dilemma quickly, Daffy." said the elf.

"Tell me the problem and I'll see if I can help?" replied Daffy.

The elf was in a hurry so he quickly explained and ran off to try and find his own solution.

Daffodil or 'Daffy' as everyone caller her suddenly jumped off the toadstool and ran to request an audience with the queen.

The queen beckoned her to enter. Daffy curtseyed and said rather excitedly, "Your majesty I think that I have found a solution to Grandma Winter's problem."

"You have?" exclaimed the queen.

"Yes I have," cried Daffy excitedly. "Well, you have seen how lovely my buttercups have grown for the children's nursery?" asked Daffy.

"Yes I certainly have and they are a credit to you. Would this have anything to do with your solution?" asked the queen.

"Oh! Yes! It does. Every morning I go down to the lake where the water lilies grow. I collect the dew drops that have fallen the night before on the floating flowers. I sprinkle the water on the garden beds. As you have seen the buttercups grow large and strong. What if we were to use some of those dew drops on Grandma Winter's rose beds? There is more than enough for our use," suggested Daffy.

The queen was delighted and asked the pixies to proclaim Daffodil the winner. Later that evening at a special ceremony the queen presented Daffodil with her reward. A bigger and better part of Fern Tree Gully's Fairyland for her to grow her new garden beds full of buttercups and blue bell flowers; a new nursery as the one she was currently working in was becoming too small.

Next day the queen sent Grunch with another letter for Grandma Winter. Grunch hurried up to the big house on Windy Hill. He clambered up the stairs rather awkwardly to ring the front door bell. When Grandma opened the front door he bowed and handed her the queen's letter then waited as instructed.

The Big House,
On Windy Hill.

Dear Grandma Winter,

I am happy to inform you that Daffodil has found a quick easy and simple answer to your problem.

If you would visit us again for afternoon tea say around 4pm, I am sure that Daffodil would delight in explaining to you her ingenious solution.

We await your arrival,
Respectfully yours,
Her Majesty,
Queen Amberlyn.

Later that afternoon Grunch and Grandma Winter made their way down to Fern Tree Gully's Fairyland through to the Fairy Queen's gardens. Her Royal Highness Queen Amberlyn and Daffy were already waiting. Grandma curtsied and again was invited by the queen to sit on the large toadstool opposite her. When Grandma Winter was seated, Queen Amberlyn asked Daffy to explain her plan.

After Daffy's speech Grandma Winter thanked her politely and commented that it was indeed just the solution that she had been looking for. Before Grandma Winter left for the Big House on Windy Hill, she had made arrangements with Daffodil to water her rose beds, with the queen's permission of course.

Several months after Daffy had begun watering Grandma Winter noticed that some of her white roses, while still retaining their beautiful scents, had begun to change colour. Some ever so slightly while others rather dramatically. Grandma talked it over with Philby but seemed to get nowhere. They just seemed to talk round and round in circles. On mentioning it to Dee Jay she began making headway.

"Do you want to know what I think?" asked Dee Jay.

"Yes, please. You know that I value any suggestions that either of you can offer," said Grandma.

"Well it could be the water that your special friends are using don't you think?" remarked Dee Jay.

"Now Grandma, why on earth didn't you think of that?" Chuckled Philby. "Well then I guess there's another visit to Fern Tree Gully coming up, eh?" He laughed as he walked out the door.

So again Grandma wrote to the fairy queen and received a reply. Grunch called at the house on Windy Hill and again clambered up the stairs awkwardly to ring the door bell. Grandma answered and together they made the usual trip down through Fairyland to the queen's gardens.

Queen Amberlyn listened and then said, "I will summon Daffodil. I am sure that she may know what is causing your white roses to change colour. The queen spoke to one of the elves who hurried off to find Daffodil.

When Daffy arrived the queen told her of Grandma's plight. Daffy stood there thinking for a moment then addressed Grandma.

"Grandma Winter, I can explain. You see when I collect the water from the brightly coloured water lilies it has been sitting there for hours. During that time the water becomes coloured with some of the colour of the particular lily it is trapped in. I have been sprinkling your roses with this coloured water and it has acted like a type of dye. Hence your roses have become coloured ones. "Are they mostly a combination of gold and orange ones?" she asked Grandma.

"Yes, they are yellow, deep gold or a combination of yellowy orange coloured ones. Some are pale yellow with very light tinges of pink on the edges of them," replied Grandma.

"That would be because I have been mainly using the water from the yellow, gold and orange lilies of which there is a greater supply. Although occasionally I have collected from the pink lilies but there are only a few of them at present," explained Daffy. "I'm sorry if I have caused you some concern. Would you prefer I didn't use the dew drops on your roses?" Daffy asked apologizing.

"Oh! No! Daffy, they are simply beautiful!" Grandma exclaimed.

Please continue as now I have not just a beautiful array of the most wonderfully scented roses but also a very special combination and an exceptional collection of the most extraordinary yellow roses." said Grandma.

Drawing Daffy closer so that her next words were only for her, "You know Daffy; yellow roses have always been my favourite. Thank you."

Iko and Coco
Friends and Saviours

Twylah and her family had just moved into a house at 46 Frangipani Drive, Rockingham Cove. Her father became chief officer of the coastguard in that sleepy little seaside village. The brick house was two stories high and from her new bedroom Twylah could see the river that ran at the back of house as far as the eye could see straight out to the ocean. While Twylah was carrying goods in from the car she stopped at the water's edge and got the fright of her life. Two dolphins jumped clear out of the water and immediately began showing off. One was up out of the water balancing on his tail. He kept moving his tail backwards and forwards by swishing it through the water. The other rolled over and over in the water all the time making pleasant sounds as if trying to communicate with Twylah. They jumped and rolled and swished their tails a few more times and then headed out to sea as if they wanted her to follow them. Soaking wet from being splashed by their antics, Twylah went to the bathroom to dry off.

In the weeks that followed Twylah established a great rapport with the dolphins. She gave them each a name. She called them Iko and Coco. They would come up the river every morning and afternoon and swim around her father's boat, the 'Sea Eagle', that he kept moored at the jetty. Twylah would feed them small fish that her father caught in the river.

Twylah loved boats and fishing and had great knowledge of both. She had learned it all from her dad. He had taught her all he knew about boats and the currents of the waters around the cove.

She was turning fifteen in a few days and her parents had surprised her with her own dinghy. They had a naming ceremony and called it 'The Sea Wolfe'. Twylah could take herself out fishing whenever she liked instead of having to wait until her father was free. For many months after school she would check all her safety gear then she would journey out into the ocean with Iko and Coco leading the way. The dolphins always did this and Twylah always felt safe when they were by her side. They would take her past the sand bar and out a short way to the ocean reef. It was their favourite feeding ground as various fish came there to feed late in the afternoon.

This afternoon Twylah and the dolphins hadn't been out long when a major storm began brewing. The threatening clouds rolled across the dark inky sky, thick and heavy. The ocean began boiling as froth and foam flew into the air and the waves crashed hard against the Sea Wolfe. Suddenly the rope that Twylah had anchoring the dinghy snapped and the boat was flung by the huge waves on to the reef with an almighty bang. By now Twylah was beginning to panic. The Sea Wolfe was taking in water and was stuck fast on the reef and to top it off the motor had snapped in two. How was she going to get home? Was she going to perish out here in freezing cold water? Twylah never stayed out in the ocean for long periods of time so she never had a radio in the dinghy. She put her life jacket on and waited as there was nothing else she could do.

The dolphins, realizing that she was in major trouble, swam around her making loud sounds while communicating with each other. At last they decided that one of them would leave Twylah and go back to her home for help while the other would stay with her. It was several hours swim to reach her home. During that time Twylah was clinging as hard as she could to her dinghy. She was hoping that Iko would make it back and be able to convince someone to follow him.

The storm raged for most of the night and as time passed Twylah was becoming increasingly scared that they would not find her. Just as dawn approached, she could hear the sound of her father's boat roaring through the water. It was now that Twylah remembered the flares amongst her safety gear. She took one out and set it off hoping that her father would see it in time. She needn't have worried as Iko has led him straight to her. In moments she was plucked from her sinking dinghy and pulled to safety on to The Sea Eagle and not a moment too soon as The Sea Wolfe began breaking up. Wet, freezing cold and exhausted, Twylah appreciated the blanket and hot tea offered. She turned to her dad and said, "I was beginning to think that I would never see any of you again. Oh! My dinghy!" she cried. "Thank you! Thank you for saving me."

Her father turned The Sea Eagle's bow about and whispered, "Come on lass it's time to go home." Everyone's anxious to see you and mum's got your dinner waiting.

The small seaside community of Rockingham Cove presented Iko and Coco with a special bravery award, a huge haul of fish, for having saved Twylah's life.

I'm Lost without You

One day two friends went to a lemonade stand and started arguing over who was going to pay. Later they went home to their mothers and asked them who should pay for the lemonade. Both mothers said the same thing.

"Take care and be kind and find your happy faces and keep it for the day."

So the two friends went to the lemonade stand and one paid for their drinks. But they were still thirsty. The other paid for another two cups.

Then the two friends went home. They told their mothers the whole story from the beginning and kept telling them for a week.

One day one of the friends had to move to a different city. They kept in touch until they were older. Ten years later one friend wrote to the other and said, "I'm moving back to your city." The other friend replied, "I'm lost without you." From then on they were able to keep in touch over the back fence.

The lesson taught: Take turns to be kind.

Joe Blake the Smart Snake
And
The Law of this Land

Until the laws changed recently, many farm households had rifles of sorts hanging on their wall and in their sheds.

With the warmer weather approaching, more than our human visitors dropped in for afternoon tea. While having coffee on the back verandah Alan jumped almost six foot high scaring all of us.

"There's a brown snake! I hate snakes! It must be four foot six inches long!" He shouted, pointing and screaming at the same time.

Helen commented that "The only good snake is a dead one."

"Damn!" said William. I'll fetch the rifle. Paddock snakes are fine but I don't like them up here around the house," he stated walking towards the shed.

Joe Blake slithered past him raising its head with a grin on its face and hissing as if to say, "Hey! Don't you know? You can't shoot me! I'm a protected species! The Law says so," as it continued its journey over to the fishpond. It almost seemed to know that our rifle is kept locked in a polished wooden case in one shed, the key that unlocks the case kept in a secret hiding place in the house and the bullets kept elsewhere.

We stood around and watched in horror as Joe Blake slithered down a hole underneath the fishpond. Suddenly its long body curled up the side and its head plunged into the water devouring two goldfish in a split second.

Before William returned, Joe Blake found another opening to plough his head into. It was an underground tunnel into the cockatiel's cage made by last night's field mice that had fed from the carpeted birdseed floor. As its head plunged through the hole a quick screech from the cockatiel and, Oops! Too late! What a fate!

After hibernating all winter the cockatiel was the snake's first major meal in months.

William arrived back in time to see a fat Joe Blake, with an even wider grin on its face, slithering over the bank at high speed down towards the bottom paddock hissing. William could almost hear it repeating itself saying, "Remember, I'm a protected species. Remember the Laws of this Land."

Katie the Garden Fairy

Once upon a time there was a garden fairy called Katie. Katie was a fairy who often wore a silky, creamy coloured blouse covered in sprays of soft pink apple blossoms. She was of medium size with sea blue eyes and had silvery gold and purple gossamer wings. Her long, flowing velvety skirt was of a softer contrasting gold and she had silver slippers adorning her dainty feet. Her long blond wind swept hair was often held in place by a delicately crafted hair clip designed by Fairyland's finest craftsmen.

Katie lived among the edge dwellers down in the gully that was situated around the outskirts of Fairyland. The gully had been formed over thousands of years by a majestic fast flowing river. As it flowed past the edge dwellers mushroom houses, this bubbly, curving, crystal clear flowing river becomes a magical waterfall. The mystical waterfall flows through Fairyland town and into a pond where the woodland ducks flock. Katie and other edge dwellers have often been seen feeding the ducks or swimming with them in the cool waters.

Around the gully and down through Fairyland itself there are a lot of odd shaped mushroom houses where the pixies, fairies and elves lived. Katie's gigantic mushroom house with its crooked windows and huge warped wooden door stood at the edge of the gully in the heart of an enormous twisted old tree. Katie loved its small, white delicate flowers. Around the front of the house, Katie planted many picturesque gardens in which grew beautiful bluebells, large buttercups and a much larger brightly coloured variety of day lilies. In the centre of each garden bed she had planted a variety of lovely pink roses which she grew especially for her grandma.

As it was lovely and sunny Katie decided that it would be a great day for a garden party. This was a grand way to share with others not just her love for gardening but also her spectacular flower beds.

"I know," Katie said, "I will invite all of Fairyland's inhabitants to my garden party so that they too may enjoy the beauty of my stunning gardens. Of course, I must not forget to invite Grandma."

When Grandma came she liked to sit on a large toadstool next to her granddaughter. All the residents of Fairyland enjoyed the soft sweet scent of the flowers as it drifted by. The young elves escorted every one to their orange and red mushroom tables and light cream and brown toadstool seats in the centre of the gardens. On Katie's instructions the elves placed on the tables, tea, fairy bread, yummy biscuits, lots of brown and white chocolate and fairy cakes covered in rainbow icing.

During the day Katie's pet donkey, Sandy, enjoyed taking the folk for rides around the gardens. Everyone who came to Katie's parties loved to dance on the thick carpet of soft, pastel green lawn while the Fairyland orchestra played their enchanting melodies. At the end of the festivities she bid farewell to everyone as they sleepily went on their way home.

In the late afternoon Katie and Grandma would often take Katie's kitten, Cheeky, (a young black panther) for long walks around the gully and down into Fairyland town itself. These long walks gave them a chance to catch up on things and chat with other people who were out and about. Before evening shadows began to fall Katie would pick her beautiful, scented pink roses for Grandma to take home.

Nature's Transformation

Every morning I wake to a kaleidoscope of colours dancing round the room as the golden sunlight gently kisses the sun crystal hanging from the window. The colours playfully dance, as it is spinning and twirling in the breeze.

Later while sitting on the veranda overlooking our paddocks, I can see on a clear day as far as the mountains.

The farms in the distance are sprinkled through out like seeds that have been blown, scattered, and dropped by the wind. It becomes an eerie sight as the misty fog slowly cloaks the mountains and slithers across engulfing all in its wake. Until farms take the shape of mountain streams and lakes. Tall trees rise above the mist dotting the countryside.

Moments pass and as the sun climbs above the trees to move stealthily across behind the misty fog I can see Nature's transformation taking place. The parched Earth becomes soaked by heavy dewdrops falling as the mist graciously drifts away leaving sections of it drenched in golden shafts of sunlight and shadows from the taller trees. The Paddocks come alive as the white owl in the old dead tree says goodnight as he nestles down for his morning sleep. Hares, rabbits and a family of quails joyfully play among the wet grasses. Field mice scurry along the ground while overhead the Eagles and Hawks circle playing in the wind-tunnels.

The large golden Wattle tree now dotted black and comes alive with the squawking of crows. Kanga Hoppers and an Ibis or two stop to nibble as they pass through. An Emu occasionally pops in to join the White Cockatoo's, Galah's, Magpie's and Butcherbirds who come to feed on the contour banks. As the cows, brolgas and scrub turkeys' drink from the water troughs natures' transformation is complete and each day becomes unique.

Pascha, Fairy Queen of Flowers

Pascha lived on the poorer side of Fairyland in a house in the woods made from the roots of an old dead tree. The house had crooked windows and a rickety door and outside was a chocolate coloured pebbled pathway scattered with small blossoms and leaves blown there by the wind.

It was almost the end of winter and all the fairies including Pascha were busily planting their trees, shrubs and flowers for the annual spring carnival. The Festival was the biggest event of the year and one that all the fairies looked forward to. They were all excited and waiting to hear who would become the next Fairy Queen. Flowers played a major part in almost every aspect of a young fairy's life. They were used for almost everything from hair decorations to the significant adornments worn by the Unicorns who lead the floats in the procession.

All the fairies were excited as the spring pageant was to be held this Saturday and one lucky fairy would be crowned Queen for the coming year. As the fairies stood around reading out the list of entrants, one fairy said, "Oh! Look! Pascha dares to enter the competition." Another fairy asked, "Who is Pascha?"

"You know, the girl who lives in that tatty old house on the edge of the woods."

"Oh! Her! Yes I know the girl. She has long blond curly hair."

"As if she could get picked to be our Fairy Queen." said a third fairy.

Pascha was standing not far away and couldn't help being upset. Pascha's mother took her aside and said, "Don't listen to them my dear as you have as good a chance as any."

Friday night a dreadful cold snap arrived and turned all the flowers white.

Oh! No! Exclaimed the fairies, there will be no colour in our carnival this year.

Pascha stepped forward and being the gentle, kind creature that she was, without hesitation said, "I can put the colour back in the flowers."

"How?" retorted the snobby fairies in response.

Pascha had been given an extraordinary gift and armed with it flew into the air and gently waved her hand over the flowers and the vibrant pink, blue, orange, yellow, red and all the other colours returned to the blooms.

That evening everyone who was anyone in the fairy world turned out for the crowning of the Fairy Queen. All the fairies were sitting on the edge of their seats hoping to hear their name called out.

"And the winner is….."

There was a pause and silence fell over the room. The announcer continued. "And the winner is Pascha for her kindness and service to the fairy community."

Pascha's mother leaned over and quietly spoke to her with gentleness in her voice. "You see, kindness is rewarded. It is not necessarily where you come from that counts."

Pascha rose from her seat and walked the red carpet to claim her crown and all the fairies began clapping. Her mother was filled with pride. Her little girl, the new Fairy Queen, sat proudly behind the Unicorns and led the procession.

What a grand day that was.

Peter the Rabbit
The Easter Bunny's Helper

It was evening and the children had been excited all day for the Easter Bunny was coming tonight. Carole put them both to bed much later than usual but they were not going to let her off. They wanted her to read them a bedtime story like she always did. They chanted together, "come on mummy Carole, tell us a story, tell us a story and then we'll go to sleep." As Chrispin was the sleepiest Carole asked him, "what do you want me to read tonight?"

Recently Grandma had bought Chrispin a fluffy bunny rabbit so Chrispin's reply was, "mummy tell me a story about my rabbit."

Carole shuffled through a few storybooks she had and couldn't find one about a rabbit. The best thing to do, she decided, was to make up one as she went along. Chrispin was rubbing his eyes which meant he was tired. She estimated that he wouldn't stay awake for much longer. Carole said to herself, "How hard can story telling be?"

Carole decided on a name for the story and the rabbit first. Armed with the title that she had created and Chrispin's bunny, she began, "Peter Rabbit, The Easter Bunny's Helper." She then continued to tell the story until the children fell asleep.

As Chrispin finally fell asleep he loosened his grip on grandma's fluffy bunny that he had been cuddling so tightly and drifted into dreamland.

Peter Rabbit hopped on to the end of Chrispin's bed and began grooming himself. Just then there was a noise at the open window and Peter spun around to see what it was. The Easter Bunny beckoned to Peter to come outside. Peter jumped to the casement and then leapt through the window and landed at the Easter Bunny's feet.

"Evening." said the Easter Bunny.

"And to you," replied Peter Rabbit.

"I wonder if you would do me a special favour, Peter."

"Oh! Of course! Always glad to help. What can I do for you?"

Tomorrow is Easter Sunday and tonight I have to deliver all these Easter eggs to all the boys and girls of the world. As a special treat I thought that it would be fun if Chrispin and Jerusha had a bunny trail to follow. It would make their Easter so much more exciting. What do you think?" queried the Easter Bunny.

"That sounds wonderful! Can I help?" asked Peter.

"Yes please! I thought that you could put these small cardboard cut-outs of my feet from their bed, through the kitchen, on to each verandah, down the stairs and out through the front garden where we will leave the first little eggs. Then past Damien's caravan and we will leave the next ones under the wooden awnings where the fairies live. Next we will lead them past the lagoon where the water lilies grow and the cascading waterfall flows down the rocks. Lastly down the path leading to the chook pen and we'll leave their baskets where the hens lay their eggs. If you'll do this for me, Peter, it would be a great help."

"I'll start now!" Peter replied excitedly.

The Easter Bunny shook Peters paw and thanked him. He then went off to finish delivering his Easter eggs to the world's children.

Peter set about making the bunny trail as the Easter Bunny instructed. He carefully tiptoed into the children's rooms to lay the cut out bunny feet on the floor. Then out through the kitchen and on to the verandahs, down the stairs and out to the front garden where he placed the first eggs in among the green grass clippings. He continued on down past Damien's caravan and into the Fairy Garden where he delivered some little eggs to the fairies under the wooden awnings. He walked around the lagoon past the floating water lilies and the waterfall and finally along the path leading to the chook pen. Once inside the pen he had to remove two chooks from their nesting pens. He took out the old grass and replaced it with fresh grass before carefully leaving their Easter baskets. Peter was pleased with himself after a job well done and was so proud to have been the Easter Bunny's helper, even if it was only for one night. He couldn't wait to see the smiling faces of the children in the morning. Peter tiptoed back into Chrispin's room and jumped up on the bed next to him and slept soundly until Easter Sunday morning.

Samantha's Rose

Logan and Samantha Chase arrived home from their honeymoon and tomorrow Logan would be back at work on the oil rig in the middle of the Arafura Sea off the coast of Darwin. Samantha drove Logan to the airport and stood sadly waving goodbye as the plane taxied down the runway.

Later that evening the plane disappeared from air controller Antonio Xavier's radar screen. All he could tell from the information was that the plane vanished somewhere near or in the Simpson Desert. Officials determined from the control tower's data that the plane may have been flying through some extremely turbulent weather. At this time of year, wild summer storms in and around that area were not unusual. Those in charge decided a rescue plane would not search until morning due to the current weather conditions.

Many hours had passed when Logan awoke soaking wet and freezing cold lying amongst the wreckage of the plane. He had a throbbing headache and when he tried to move he felt a sharp pain in his right shoulder. As light appeared in the sky he could see the open gashes to his left leg and ankle. Because of the severity of these injuries he collapsed with a massive fever. He fell in and out of consciousness and had wild frightening dreams. He dreamt of black men with white beards wearing no clothes and carrying long spears. He also dreamt of water, Samantha, wedge-tailed eagles and deep blood-red roses although not in any particular order that he could make any sense of.

In actuality, there were black men with him who spent several days healing his wounds by using bush medicine. They would be there when he woke from time to time then they would disappear. This happened several times a day.

After Logan's fever broke he was still laying among the wreckage. He discovered that his wounds were healed. How? He remembered dreaming about six black men with white beards. Was it just a dream? He was not sure.

He limped over to what was left of the front of the plane to find the pilot still trapped in the twisted metal. He had died instantly on impact. Sitting on the seat next to the pilot was a shoulder bag which held some food. It consisted of some sandwiches, three pieces of fruit and a large bottle of water. As Logan picked it up he thought, "It's no use to him now. I'm sure he won't mind."

For the first time, Logan realized that he was lost in the desert, alone and injured. He looked around but there was no sign of the strange black men so he turned his attention to the wreckage and began looking for anything that could be useful to him. He found a shard of glass from the front of the plane and a piece of sharp metal that he could use for cutting. He looked for his suitcase as earlier that morning Samantha had packed it with the usual items anyone would have when they are living miles away from home. He finally found it having to move debris to get to it. This was slow and painful because although his other wounds had healed his right shoulder hadn't. Opening his suitcase he removed a mirror and a razor from his toilet bag. He changed his short sleeved t-shirt and shorts for a long sleeved shirt and long pants. He didn't know much about the desert except that it reached hot temperatures during the day and could be freezing at night.

After rummaging through the rest of his suitcase he found his compass, a warm jumper, a clean pair of socks, another two long sleeved shirts, jeans and his old weather-beaten hat. After he had found everything of use he crammed as much as possible into the shoulder-bag and placed the food on top. Logan used one of the belts from his jeans to strap his right arm to his body finding this a little less painful and a bit more comfortable. He placed the bag on his left shoulder and took out his compass and, not being at all sure where he was, began walking in a north westerly direction.

In the mean time, on the morning of the day after the plane went down, Samantha was woken by the ringing of the telephone. The call she received was from the airline informing her that the plane carrying her husband to the oil rig had crashed somewhere in or around the Simpson Desert. She was in shock as the official tried to reassure her that they were doing everything possible. A search and rescue team had left at first light to try and find the plane. All Samantha could do was try and keep calm while she waited for news.

The rescue plane scoured the outskirts and centre of the desert but they made no sightings.

Then a week had passed and officials believed that everything that could possibly be done to locate the plane had been done. All their efforts had turned up nothing so they called off the search. When Samantha heard the news she was devastated and begged them to continue. They explained that a search and rescue was very costly, however, if there was a glimmer of hope that anyone was still alive, then the search would continue. He reminded her that there had been no sightings after a week of searching.

Logan had walked several miles but the sun was relentless and there was no shade. Painfully, he lay down on a sand dune. He took a couple of sandwiches, some fruit and water from his shoulder bag very much aware that food and water was scarce out here in the desert so he had to ration what he had if he was to survive the ordeal. The sun was high in the sky telling Logan it was midday and he knew he needed to rest during the hottest part of the day conserving his strength then moving on when evening approached. Because of the heat he spread one of his shirts over the sand and laid down placing the other shirt over the top of him. He pulled his hat down to cover his face and tried to sleep. The heat from the dunes and the force of the wind whipping up the sand made it impossible to sleep. The pain in his shoulder was relentless as was the golden ball of fire hanging high in the sky. Late in the afternoon he had another sip of water and finally fell asleep.

Logan awoke after having some more frightening dreams about the black men. The hot sun had gone and, as the evening rapidly approached he was left with a large glowing moon, freezing temperature and ice-cold wind. As he rose the shifting sand dune moved underneath him. Finally he staggered to his feet and placed the food and water back into his shoulder bag. He put the spare clothes on to try to get warm. Then he was ready to move on again. He was lucky as that night there was a full moon to help him with his compass bearings. Logan hoped he was heading in the right direction to find a supply of water and hopefully a town nearby. As he wandered in the desert he often had the feeling that someone or something was watching and following him. What? Why? On some nights the deep dark blackness meant he could only walk several miles as he had no moonlight to show the way. When he stopped to rest he wondered if he would be rescued or if he would die alone out here in the desert. The natural will to live and thoughts of his beautiful wife, Samantha, gave him the strength to go on. Lost, alone and injured his dreams were always the same. He would wake shivering and ringing wet with sweat.

Samantha was surrounded by her family and friends. Without their help she could not have made it through the weeks that followed Logan's disappearance. It seemed like she was in a living nightmare. Her family and friends kept her busy which made the waiting a little more bearable.

Logan had been wandering out in the desert for almost a fortnight and he was beginning to believe that he would never see his beloved Samantha again. Little did he know that Samantha had started to believe the same about him.

Walking several miles every night he had managed to find some small waterholes but no town. His spirits were low and he began to become disorientated. By now he was hungry and would have given anything for a juicy steak, however, he did manage to find a few small lizards. The first few days he would let them go but as his hunger grew he found a way to eat them. Logan thought that he could hear faint laughter in the distance but saw nothing.

Sometimes he was heading north and sometimes south. His eyes wouldn't focus properly to be able to read the bearings and this made it more difficult for him. Because of his drifting in different directions he didn't realize that he had crossed the Simpson Desert from one state to the other. His plane went down near the Queensland, South Australian and Northern Territory borders. He did not know that he was in Conservation Park and not still in the Simpson Desert.

Logan was in a weak state, tired, dirty, hungry and in pain. His feet were swollen and blistered and this made it difficult to walk so he was not making as much progress as he had previously. He staggered to his feet once more knowing that if he did not keep going, no matter how slowly, he would surely die. He took out his compass and, adjusting his eyes to see the right bearings, he set off in a north-westerly direction. He thought he could hear faint talking in the distance again and could feel a presence but still could not see anyone. He didn't know what to make of it.

All this time Samantha patiently sat by the telephone hoping that someone would ring saying that her husband had been sighted but she knew it was wishful thinking. Although her relatives crowded around with much love and support, it didn't really help. She missed Logan desperately and sat staring at the door hoping that he would walk in at any moment. With each passing minute her despair became deeper and deeper.

Not having any idea where he was, Logan found himself in some forest where he did something that under normal circumstances would be inconceivable to him. As he was stumbling around he came across some wild dogs that had killed an older dog and were settling in to tear it apart. Logan, without any regard for his safety, picked up a large branch and yelling at the top of his voice ran at the dogs and drove them away. He dragged the carcass away to a safe distance hoping the other dogs wouldn't come back. Again, he heard the voices and chuckles in the distance.

He scooped up some leaves and light twigs and holding the mirror he had retrieved from his suitcase used the rays of the sun to start a fire. Then he used the piece of metal to cut a leg from the dead dog. He put two forked branches on either side of the fire and pushed a stick through the dog's leg and placed it on the divided branches over the fire to cook it. When he had finished eating he turned to the dog and said, "You know, you were finger licking good. The best meal I've had in about three weeks mate. Thank you." His sense of humor returned for the first time since the crash.

Each day was the same, sleeping during the day and walking during the night. The walking had become slower and slower and the pain more severe. It had been almost four weeks now and he had not stumbled across any town or sign of civilization. He was now heading due north again which took him over the border into the Northern Territory and was back in the desert again. Using the compass he decided to go directly east hoping this would bring him closer to something. Anything would be preferable from the desert. Sounds echoed quietly from the distance and the sense of some presence was stronger. The echoes were telling him that this was not the right direction but he tried to ignore them. The echoing seemed to become more forceful so finally he decided to change direction again and head west. This seemed to appease the distant echoing sounds.

Logan stood up as tall as he could and placed his hand over his eyes and stared at what he thought was water with a few trees surrounding it. "Is it? Can it be? No! Surely not! My eyes are playing tricks on me," he thought. But, there it was; a waterhole on the edge of the desert. It looked like a mini Billabong. He half stumbled and half ran then threw himself into the cool water and drank and drank. He washed the sand from his face and clothes then settled down to rest while the sun was high in the sky again.

Another week had passed and Logan still sat at the water hole and wondered what to do and in what direction to go. All of a sudden he noticed the beautiful rosebush with its one lonely flower pointing north-west and wondered why he had not seen it before now. Next a vision of Samantha entered his head. Not knowing why, he looked up and saw four huge wedge tail eagles soaring high in a north-westerly direction. Now he realized the meaning of his dreams. His spirit lifted and he believed that Samantha had sent the eagles to guide him home. In minutes he had packed up his few belongings and using the piece of metal carefully dug around the rosebush, scooped it up and wrapped it in several large leaves and after watering the plant and filling his water bottle from the billabong he proceeded in the direction that the eagles were flying.

Eventually the echoing sounds became fainter and then stopped. The sensation of something or someone following him had also disappeared. The black men with white beards, no clothes and long spears who had healed his wounds knew it was time for them to leave. He was now on the right trail that would lead him to a town and eventually home.

After another four days the eagles had led him to a small town called Rumbalara where he stopped and looked around. From where he stood the whole town consisted of one roadhouse, three people and a dog but he didn't mind. It was great! Here he was in a town. Civilization again at last! He limped slowly down the main street and into the roadhouse. The first thing he asked the ruby-haired woman behind the counter was, "Where's ya telephone lovie?"

She replied, "In case you hadn't noticed ducky we live in the middle of nowhere. We ain't got no telephones out here."

"I suppose you don't have newspapers either?" he asked.

"Yeah, we got papers, they are usually three months behind but we do get them eventually," was her sarcastic reply.

Logan decided that he was getting nowhere fast with her so he walked back outside. Just then a fuel tanker pulled up to off-load some of his cargo. Logan got talking to the driver and discovered that he was headed to Alice Springs. Then he was off home for a few days before starting the run again. The truckie stood back and eyed Logan inquisitively. "Gees' mate, you look a bit worse for wear. What happened?" he asked.

"It's a long story," he replied. "You wouldn't like some company on the way to Alice Springs would you?"

"Long stories are best told over a hearty breakfast. Care to join me?"

It had been a while since Logan had eaten and the way he felt he could eat a horse and chase its rider too so he didn't hesitate to take the truckie up on his offer. After breakfast the truckie helped Logan up into the rig and after the ruby-haired woman signed for the delivery they were on the road towards Alice Springs. Having now heard Logan's story, the driver radioed ahead to the local hotel in Alice Springs asking them to relay a message to the local police.

After being on the road for another two days they arrived in Alice Springs. The local police were there to meet him and he went with them to the station where he related his story to them and anyone who wanted to listen. The police contacted the airline, the oil rig and Samantha to let them know that Logan had survived the crash.

Due to his poor condition and his injuries, he was admitted to the Alice Springs hospital. The doctor on duty told Logan that by the look of the scars on his forehead, left leg and ankle they had been badly infected at some stage and he was lucky they had not turned gangrenous. "How did you manage to heal them when you were so far away from any help?" asked the doctor.

"I don't know replied Logan. He was not sure whether to tell him about the mysterious black men. They would probably think he had imagined it while he was delirious. "Better to keep this experience to myself for now," he thought.

"Because of your exposure to the elements and your broken collarbone, it could be a few more days before you go home so lie back and enjoy the rest. You have earned it." said the doctor.

One evening the ringing of the phone seemed louder and more urgent than usual and as someone went to answer it, Samantha started screaming hysterically. As she held her face in her hands she yelled at the top of her voice, "Oh! My God! Oh! My God! It's Logan. He's alive! He's alive!" Her hands were shaking as she took the phone and hearing Logan's voice was music to her ears. She was ecstatic as she turned to her family and friends. "He's alive! He walked miles for days and weeks to end up at a roadhouse in a place called Rumbalara. A truckie drove him to Alice Springs where he was admitted to the hospital and according to the doctors he will be there for a few more days because of his injuries. I don't mind how long it takes for him to recover, he's alive and that's all that matters. Up till now I thought I had lost him forever."

Next morning she got a call from the oil rig telling her that they would fly her out to Alice Springs to be with her husband. It was just the best news. Samantha had missed Logan so much during his disappearance and she knew she never wanted to be apart from him again.

As Logan and Samantha left the Alice Springs hospital, the media were here to greet them. Logan didn't know how many times he told his story over the following months. He still believed that while he was in the desert the distant sounds he heard from the black men were real and that they looked after him. He also believed that Samantha sent the rosebush and the eagles to show him the way home.

In a warm sunny place in the back garden, Samantha and Logan planted the blood-red and black rose which Logan named in honour of his beloved wife. At the naming ceremony with family and friends in attendance, Logan watered the rose saying gently, "from now on I hereby name you 'Samantha's Rose'."

The Fairy Princess's Enchanted Butterfly Garden

Once upon a time in a faraway land there lived a very happy beautiful young princess named Jerusha. She had sea blue eyes, delicate pink, gold and lavender gossamer butterfly wings and curly golden hair.

Each morning pretty white doves would bring her a stunning wreath of the palest pink and light blue bell flowers from the enchanting forest nearby to wear in her hair.

In the early morning dew her beautiful pink and gold dress would glisten in the filtered sunlight.

Sometimes she would sit outside her little mushroom house on a gigantic pink toadstool in the peaceful gardens filled with red roses, white daisies and deep blue violets reading her favourite stories to Mrs. Rabbit.

The fairy princess had many favourite pastimes. One was to play and dance around outside in her golden slippers.

But her most favourite was when she had afternoon tea in the enchanted garden with her beloved mother and grandmother.

In the late afternoon they would sit together in the enchanted butterfly garden on small mushrooms stools under the huge plum tree.

The fairy princess would gather and place assorted leaves on the large toadstool table then watch while her mother placed on the same table, cakes covered with soft lemon and cherry icing. Her grandmother would gracefully pour sweet scented lemon tea into the cups.

While they chatted, ate and sipped their tea, brightly coloured butterflies and fireflies flitted around in the cool afternoon breeze. Grasshoppers, snails, beetles and ants rustled in the mulch underneath their feet waiting for any crumbs to fall.

Grandmother would leave as evening approached and as the sun began to set, the fairy princess and her mother retired awaiting the dawning of another bright and new exciting day.

HOOT OWL.   E. NIESLER

The Folk of Fern Tree Gully

Ring! Ring!

"Hello," said Grandma North. "Hello mum, can Carissa come to stay for the school holidays?" asked Carole. "Yes, she's always welcome," replied Grandma.

"If we leave now we'll be there by three," said Carole.

"Right, we'll expect you then." replied Grandma.

Carole and Carissa arrived on time and after a small amount of pleasantries and a quick bite of afternoon tea, Carole was on her way again. "Sorry mum. Must fly, I'm working tomorrow. Bye darling. Make sure you are good for Grandma. Love you." she called out the window as she drove away.

Eight year-old Carissa stood there with her sad moon shaped face, soft brown hair and hazel eyes looking up at Grandma.

Grandma said, "Cheer up. It's too late now but tomorrow Poppy will take you down to meet the folk of Fern Tree Gully who live in our forest."

Next morning Carissa woke to the sound of parrots and happy jacks singing and playing in the trees outside.

Poppy drove Carissa to the contour bank at the far end of the paddock. "Take my hand; you don't want to get lost. When we step over this bank we'll be in the forest. Hurry Carissa," shouted Poppy. "We might just be in time to catch Hoot Owl before he goes to bed."

Walking through the forest Carissa could see the beautiful large leafy ferns that grew as big as trees and the giant mushrooms with their funny little windows and doors. This was where the good fairies lived. There was a thick carpet of peat covering the ground and a clear running stream that shone like crystal in the sunlight. They stopped at a dead hollow tree where Hooty Owl lived.

Poppy pointed and said, "Look, Carissa. There's Hooty Owl."

"Hooty, off to bed now?" asked Poppy.

"Yes. Well that's the evening shift done." Replied Hooty as he nestled inside his tree.

Just then a family of field mice and some quails scurried past to hide in the long grasses whispering, "The foxes are coming."

Albi is a well groomed male fox with a white chest and golden fur. He was quite large compared to Chestnut, his mate. Together they patrolled the boundaries making sure the little folk were protected. These included the lion cat Simba, ducks floating on the stream, Bandy the rooster and his girls foraging amongst the peat, kanga hoppers and cows all wandering through. Lady Hawk circled the skies playing in the wind currents but ever alert for any impending danger.

A flock of black-red tailed parrots and some kookaburras flew overhead laughingly telling Poppy that it would rain in a few days.

This was only the beginning so Carissa felt sure she was going to have a magical holiday.

The Geriatrics Disastrous Fishing Trip

It was Wednesday and another week had passed. Phil was heading up the road for his usual pot of ale or two, raffles and a friendly chat with the 'geriatric boys'.

Ces who suffered from chronic arthritis was the oldest and the best fisherman by far. All agreed he could catch a fish in a bucket. Next was Phil who suffered from gout and was the owner and driver of the boat. He would pack the boat on Friday afternoon in order to be ready when the others rocked up at six that night. Terry or 'Doctor Who', as he was affectionately known was the third member. He qualified because he suffered from osteoarthritis in his neck and wore a long multi-coloured scarf to keep it warm. He would spend the entire journey complaining about how painful it was but he would never miss a trip.

Once a week all three would gather at their favourite watering hole to talk over the misadventures of their last fishing trip and to begin planning their next. They all expected it to be the same as usual but none of them were prepared for what was about to happen this time round.

By now the ales were beginning to take effect and the stirring about last week's mishaps began.

"This time, Doctor Who, when you climb aboard, try and remember to put the bungs in position." said Phil.

"Yeah!" said Ces, "or you'll be bailing out the water yourself."

Of course he was quicker than a fish to bite. "Now listen fellas, no listen," raising his voice above their taunting. "It wasn't my fault. It really wasn't," he said laughingly, "I simply just forgot."

The others stood there shaking their heads in disbelief at his reply and laughing.

"It's no wonder that other fishermen call us the Geriatric Crew." Chirped Phil and Ces in unison.

All three lived for their fishing so it wasn't unusual for Friday afternoon to take a long time coming around, but, at last it arrived and they had all turned up on time to find Phil admiring the beautiful sunset.

Ces called out, "Come on, we've got better things to do than watch the sun set."

"Hurry up, we're ready to go." Shouted Doctor Who.

"Well for one thing I'm not just watching the sun set. You know what they say don't you? 'Red in the morning, shepherds' warning, red at night, shepherds delight.' Look closely at the sky Ces and you'll find a shepherds' delight which means a good trip," was Phil's comeback.

Originally the boat was called the 'Sea Wolfe' but was given the nickname The Geriatric Society' by other fishermen referring to all the ailments of those who sailed on her. They all made a last check of everything and Ces said, "All we need now is go go juice when we get to Rosalea Bay."

Eagerly they all piled into the car never realizing the disasters about to befall them. They were in a jolly mood as Phil drove up the main drag. He was too busy talking to Doctor Who to notice that the lights ahead had changed to amber not giving him enough time to stop. Because of the size and weight of the boat he would have to continue on and run a red light.

"Damn," said Phil, "how unlucky can you be? I've never run a red light before."

"First time for everything mate," said Ces. Their laughter soon ceased when they heard the police siren and saw his flashing lights in the rearview mirror.

"Pull over please." The police officer instructed and Phil pulled up to the side of the road.

The police officer asked Phil to get out of the car then asked, "What is your full name please?"

"Phillip Ronald Baker," he answered.

"Well Mr. Baker you have just run a red light so may I see your drivers licence? Have you been drinking today sir?"

Phil answered yes and no accordingly.

"Your licence please?" the officer asked again.

Phil fumbled around in the glove box then said, "I've left it at home officer."

"In that case you have twenty four hours to present it at the nearest police station." He took out his book and began an inspection of the car, trailer and boat.

"Well aren't you the lucky one? A new car is it? No faulty tyres, dents or scratches and the boat and trailer are in good order, too. We take good care of everything do we? It's a shame that we don't take as much care on the roads. I'll have to book you on that offence alone," he said sarcastically as he tore the ticket from his book and handed it to Phil. "You have a nice day now." He said as he walked back to his car. Phil turned to Doctor Who waving the ticket saying jokingly, "this is all your fault so you should pay for it!"

Doctor Who replied, "It could have been worse so stop your grizzling."

Everything was going smoothly again until they passed through La Moore Beach. As they came up to the tiny roundabout at Statute Bay, Ces let out a yell. "Phil, look out!" Phil swerved quickly, running almost over the edge of the embankment knowing he would not have seen the other car at the last minute if it hadn't been for Ces's warning.

Phil sat with his hands still shaking on the steering wheel. As the other drive walked over to him Phil shouted, "You fool, what do you think you were doing? You could have killed us all!"

"I…. I'm sorry," he said apologetically. "What can I say? There's no real harm done."

After Phil calmed down they headed off again and finally arrived at Rosalea Bay and Phil declared, "I can't wait to get out to sea, it's a damn sight safer out there."

Ces and Doctor Who replied, "Our sentiments exactly."

As Phil backed the car down the ramp he heard an enormous thump then felt a huge jerk. He slammed on the brakes and got out to see what had happened.

"The safety chain broke," shouted Ces.

"Damn," Phil yelled at the top of his voice, "can anything else go wrong today?"

Finally they were on their way heading out through the bay to their favourite fishing ground. They left the harbour in good spirits despite all the happenings never dreaming that the worst disaster was yet to come.

Doctor Who, barely waiting for the boat to stop baited up and dropped his line over the side. Seeing this, Phil calls, "Ay! Good one mate! Where's the tinnies, hey?" While they were preparing their lines Doctor Who reached into the esky replying, "Sorry mate." Then they all settled back in quiet anticipation of the first catch of the day.

Their thoughts were of catching some Red Emperor, Sweet Lip and Dew fish, some of the ocean's most precious jewels. Ces started the argument off again as usual. "As you got the jump start on us Doctor Who I thought you'd be reeling them in by now." Just then he felt a tug on his line and shouted triumphantly, "We're away now fellas! It must be at least an eighty pound one!" Coming to give him a hand they both began laughing hysterically for dangling from his line was a baby toadfish that even when it puffed itself up was no bigger than eight centimeters in diameter.

Phil exclaimed, "Doctor Who you've excelled yourself this time mate. Heck, that one must weigh at least ninety pounds, hey Ces?"

"Yeah, mate yeah," replied Ces jokingly. Then Ces brought his line to the surface and dangling from the end was the head of a Red Emperor so Doctor Who seeing his chance for a little fun and revenge at the same time shouted to Ces. "Hey mate! That's the best one yet! It's even bigger than mine!" Phil was too busy to comment and continued dragging his line to the surface. "Now fellas," Phil said teasingly, "that's the way you do it," poking the big Dew fish under their noses.

Phil always turned on the radio just before seven to catch the evening news and the next day's weather forecast. "And now for tonight and tomorrow's weather," the announcer said. Phil shouted, "Ssh! You pair, I want to hear this."

The weather will be fine tomorrow with a light north-west breeze blowing at about eight to ten knots. There is a high pressure system building in the Bight, but it is not expected to have any effect on our weather for at least another two or three days."

"I'll be damned if I know where they get their 'light' breeze from as it would have to be blowing at least ten knots already," commented Ces angrily.

"Yeah, and how many times have we heard the Coast Guard state that some of their rescues wouldn't have had to take place if only the owner had kept a closer eye on the weather?" replied Doctor Who.

As they continued fishing, the boat started to really rock and roll, as the breeze began to slowly pick up to fifteen knots causing the sea to swell.

Later in the evening they all decided to bunk down for the night. Phil always made his bed on the top of the engine box so he could keep an eye on the anchor and the direction the boat was drifting. Phil believed that when you're out at sea, a good fisherman is like a good sailor who sleeps with one eye open. He had a restless night and, before the morning broke, was awakened by a huge gush of water pouring in over the stern. The anchor rope had snapped off and the 'Geriatric Society' was beginning to drift. He jumped to his feet as the craft rocked and rolled aimlessly in the water. He shouted to the others, "She's going to sink if we don't get things under control."

As they all tried desperately to stop themselves from crashing on to the rocks, Ces stared at the red streaks in the blackened sky and his thoughts went back to Phil's remarks of the previous day. "Red in the morning, shepherd's warning."

Phil fought his way back to the cabin and began calling the Coast Guard. "May Day! May Day! This is Gum Nut Two calling VJ4YN. Over! If anyone can hear us our boat the 'Sea Wolfe' is being forced onto rocks in gale force winds and seas four metres high." Almost immediately there was a faint reply. "Hello! Gum Nut Two this is VJ4YN. We are checking to see if there are any other vessels in your immediate area that may be able to assist you."

"Gum Nut Two this is Peter Pan One. We heard your call for help and are on our way to assist. How bad is your situation? Over."

"Peter Pan our situation is becoming quite grave."

"Will it be possible to tow you in?"

"Negative, Peter Pan, the Sea Wolfe is being pounded against the rocks and is breaking up. Hurry! Please hurry!"

Because of the fierce winds, driving rain and monstrous waves pounding against the rocks, it was difficult for Peter Pan One to get close enough. As the last man was plucked from the sea the Coast Guard arrived and escorted Peter Pan One back to port.

The drive home went without incident.

Phil was woken by a loud banging on the front door next morning and opened it to find two police officers standing there. One asked, "Are you Mr. Baker?"

"Yes." Phil replied.

In that case sir, please explain your failure to present your licence within the required time." Phil began to laugh and the officer remarked, "Oh! You find that amusing do you?"

Phil shook his head and explained. "This is incredible! I have just lost my boat and almost my life and those of my crew and all you're worried about is my damn drivers licence!"

E. NIESLER.

The Little Leprechaun

As Shamus walked into his favourite place 'The Shamrock' Pat O'Leary cried out, "Hey! Shamus, tell us again how you captured a little Leprechaun." "Tell us again how he got away." Shamus ignored the laughs and gestures from others. Instead he began with, "Ah! Ha! Me wee lads and pretty colleens, gather ye round and I'll tell you the story of the time I caught a wee Leprechaun."

He then settled in and proceeded to tell the tale.

"Back in old Ireland in the days of yore it is said that there lived a little wee man who's seldom seen anymore. He was the master of magic and considered to be the best in the land. He stood six inches high and always dressed in green. He had short snowy white curly hair which complimented his long pointy beard that curled upwards when it reached his plump middle.

"With the bluest of eyes he would wink at you from underneath his thick bushy eyebrows. He wore a big silver buckled belt around his plump little waist. A long stemmed emerald green shamrock protruded from the black trim of his green pixie-like hat. Golden bells that jangled when he walked hung from the end of his hat and his dainty pixie slippers. As he skipped through the leafy tree and fern covered dells you could hear him singing-

'Fiddly diddly, catch a min-a-me quick or I'll be gone,

Fiddly diddly, catch a min-a-me I'm a Leprechaun.'

"The legend of the little Leprechaun has been passed down over the centuries and when I was a wee child I remember more than once being told the story of the Little Leprechaun and his crop of gold. He would stash his pot of golden sovereigns at the end of a brightly coloured rainbow. It is said by many that if you can catch one of these wee little men then he would grant you a wish. Catching this wee little man was a lot harder than it sounded. Whenever I would see him he would be sitting in the forest on a hollowed out tree stump. More than once I tried to creep up on him but he would disappear with a laugh singing his little rhyme-

'Fiddly diddly, catch a min-a-me quick or I'll be gone,

Fiddly diddly, catch a min-a-me I'm a Leprechaun.'

"One night while walking through the woods I could see a small fire. I thought that I would get closer just to have me a peek. Gradually I crept closer and closer and to my surprise I saw a score of little Leprechauns who were happily dancing around the fire singing-

'Fiddly diddly, catch a min-a-me quick or I'll be gone,

Fiddly diddly, catch a min-a-me I'm a Leprechaun.'

"I decided to sit down and wait until they had finished dancing and having their fun and when they went to sleep then maybe I would have a chance to catch me one. At last they were weary and exhausted from their dancing and singing so they lay down beside a huge log to sleep. Rubbing my hands together I thought now I'll catch me one and his crop of gold and a special wish will be all mine. I crept slowly over and grabbed one very tightly but he turned into a frog. He was all wet and slippery and sprang from my hands. As he hopped away through the leafy woods I could hear him singing-

'Fiddly diddly, catch a min-a-me quick or I'll be gone,

Fiddly diddly, catch a min-a-me I'm a Leprechaun.'"

As Shamus finished his tale some of the crowd dispersed but the taunting continued from those who remained.

When Shamus had had enough he went home.

E. NIESLER

The Pumpkin Twin Fairies

Once upon a time Granny Appleseed, Anci and Puttsy lived near the sparkling crystal springs in The Rainbow Fern Forrest.

Granny welcomed Anci into her home when she was just a baby along with her little dog Puttsy. Anci and Puttsy were inseparable. Anci was an impressionable and sweet little child of seven years with long curly raven black hair.

All through the years Granny spent many hours telling Anci about when she was a child. Her aunts had told her about the fairies, pixies and elves that lived in their separate little villages' at the bottom of the beautiful garden but Granny's mother didn't believe the stories. She told Anci of the big old twisted willow tree in the back yard and the fairy folk that lived in it and the dark caves that were held together by its curling roots.

Granny Appleseed told her stories of the Mushroom Village with its curving streets and the dark pools where Old Spinner lived. Ants were a favourite of Old Mr. Prickles who lived in a hole in the ground near by. The fairies would serve delicious Moth Cakes and Ant cookies and in leafy flower cups, dandelion tea or warm nectar collected from the bumble bees. She spoke often of the small fairy shops where fairy folk shopped like normal people. She described the waterfall that flowed into the ferny glades where the elves lived in their extra large Toadstool houses. And of beautiful butterfly carriages that take you high over the mountains to the Fairy King and Queen's Place.

"Granny," asked Anci one day, "when can I go to see this mushroom village and the fairy folk that you speak about so often?"

"Anci," explained Granny, "you must find and follow the secret cobbled path hidden by drooping large ferns and mossy covered boulders. The cobbled path winds its way alongside the sparkling stream till you come to the old twisted willow tree. There you will find a large pale green door just visible. If you wait there quietly you will find the fairies will come out to play with you. But Anci you must truly believe that they exist."

"Oh! Granny I do!" Exclaimed Anci rather excitedly.

"If the fairies fail to come then you could always go through Mr. Prickles' hole in the ground," suggested Granny.

"Anci! Promise me that you will remember never to go looking for the Fairies pot of gold at the end of their brightly coloured rainbows that glow like crystals in the sunlit sky after heavy showers of rain," asked Granny rather sternly.

"Why, Granny? Wouldn't the fairies pot of gold be your reward for looking after me and Puttsy?" asked Anci.

"No! Anci. It wouldn't! So you stay away from the crystal rainbows that hang in the sunlit sky because they can be funny things you know. If you ever get caught under one you will never be able to come home again," replied Granny.

The start of the school holidays had been rather bleak. Heavy rain had been falling for more that a week. By now Anci and Puttsy were more than bored. They wanted to run and play outside in the warm sunshine. Their chance came at last when Granny finally allowed them to go outside and play.

As Anci and Puttsy skipped on the slightly wet grass they could hear Granny calling, "You look after Anci and don't let her stray too far from home now Puttsy wont you?"

"Now Puttsy I have a plan," Said Anci. "Let's go and find granny's cobbled path that will lead us into the fairies special world."

"Woof, Woof," replied Puttsy jumping about rather excitedly.

So off they went running around looking for the cobbled path hidden by droopy large ferns and mossy covered boulders. All of a sudden Anci ran right into Old Spinners web. A sharp prick from Old Spinners pincers and Anci slipped and hit her head on the mossy covered boulders. And Oops! Unconscious Anci followed closely by Puttsy falls into Mr. Prickles' hole in the ground. She fell straight on top of Mr. Prickle's luscious food store of ants. Groggy and groaning for a short second she opens her eyes to see a pair of twin pumpkins. To her they looked identical in size with finely pale pink gossamer wings. Then back to sleep she goes.

Just then Mr. Prickles wandered in. "Oh! My goodness! What do we have here?" Exclaimed Mr. Prickles in fright. The Spiny Ant Eater hadn't seen too many human children before. As Mr. Prickles bent down to pick up Anci, Puttsy growled, showed his small white teeth and barked loudly at him. Ignoring him Mr. Prickles placed her on his lacy bed covers made of ant's legs from the finest ant hills around The Rainbow Fern Forest.

"Who is she? And why does she visit me?" thought Mr. Prickles to himself. "What do I do with her?"

Mr. Prickles prodded and poked her but she wouldn't wake up. He looked closer and found a rather large bump on her forehead and a little prick hole surrounded by a reddish tinge

"Oh! My dear! It looks like Old Spinner got you. I must find the fairies for they'll know what to do."

While Mr. Prickles wandered off to find the fairies Puttsy not really knowing what to do settled down next to Anci laying his head across her chest. Mr. Prickles finally surfaced from his underground tunnel next to the cobbled pathway leading to the Fairies village. He continued to swagger along slowly at an even pace for he knows that time is of the essence. He must find the fairies soon so that they can find an antidote to Old Spinner's poison.

By now Anci was in a deep sleep and as the fever took hold of her she kept dreaming. She dreamt about the two little twin pumpkins with their pale pink gossamer wings. These pumpkins had taken the shape of small plump orangey yellow fairy children who still had pale pink gossamer wings. They began to speak to her in quite tones.

"Anci today is our annual pumpkin festival would you like to come? There will be lots to see and do. You can even roll us down the pumpkin hill." Drowsily Anci replied, "Yes! I would like to come but I am too weak so how will I get there?

The pumpkins replied, "Just place your hand one each side of us and we will fly there."

Next thing the pumpkins and Anci with Puttsy hanging on to Anci's legs (for fear of falling from great heights) were flying over the cobbled pathway with its drooping large ferns and mossy covered boulders. Up, up they flew over the old twisted willow tree, over the dark caves and the cool waterfall past the ferny glades where the Elves lived in their Toadstool houses down into Goomeri that special part of the fairies village where the festival was held every year.

Anci, supported each side by the sprightly walking orangey yellow pumpkins with their pale pink gossamer wings and followed closely by Puttsy wandered around part of the fairies' village on this fine fuzzy day. They walked around the curving streets looking at all the pumpkin people and their stalls. The pumpkin stall was selling flower and leafy cups. Others had fine silver gossamer doilies spun from the finest thread that Old Spinner could make. Delicious Moth Cakes and Ant Cookies were sold along with dandelion tea or sweet honey nectar from the bumble bees trees. The village was a hive of activity. In another part of town Anci could see all the fairy folk bustling around like normal people from fairy shop to fairy shop. At last they came to the pumpkin roll hill. Anci struggled to the top assisted by her two twin pumpkin friends. As the other pumpkins took their place the man with the gun said, "ready, set, go!"

They all started rolling down the hill. Next thing Anci knew, she, the pumpkin twins and Puttsy had some how rolled back into Mr. Prickles' hole. Sleep over took her once more.

Later but how much later Anci didn't know but she could hear faint voices. It was Mr. Prickles and some of the fairy folk who had come to help. The fairy nurse said, "She's from the human world. How did she find her way here? We must find a way to help her and return her to the human world before they discover her gone."

Another fairy nurse suggested, "We must go and consult with Old Spinner. Surely he will know an antidote that will cure her."

"I'll stay and try to make her a little more comfortable," said Mr. Prickles.

Off flew the fairies in great haste to see Old Spinner. The fairies landed on his silvery silken web each one side of him.

"Hey!" said Old Spinner loudly, "who dares to disturb my siesta?"

"It is the fairy nurses," replied the fairies in unison. "Mr. Prickles has himself a dilemma," continued one fairy.

"He has found a human child in his burrow that has been bitten by a spider. Mr. Prickles thinks it was you."

Do you know of a cure for your poison?" inquired the other fairy. Together they said to Old Spinner that, "we must find a cure quickly and return her to the human world before she is discovered missing."

"Yes. There is a cure," replied Old Spinner. "But it is far away in the fiery purple dragon's realm. "You must fly high over the mountains and past the ferny glades where the waterfalls fall gently. Then into the dark twisted caves where the wee yellow dew drop flowers grow. But mind you look out for the old purple dragons for they will fry you if they can," warned Old Spinner with a hearty chuckle.

"Thank you," the fairies called as they flew away.

The fairies told Mr. Prickles what Old Spinner has said.

"No offence Mr. Prickles," said the fairies, "but you cannot go for you would be too slow. Who do we know who can fly high and be fast enough not to be caught by the purple dragons?"

"I know," said Mr. Pickles. "I can ask Mr. Benjamin Wedge Tail Eagle. He flies fast and high in the sky and is definitely fast enough not to be caught. Come outside and I will call him."

Mr. Pickles placed his fingers over his lips and blew as hard as he could. Within minutes Mr. Benjamin Wedge Tail Eagle arrived.

Mr. Pickles began to tell Mr. Benjamin the tale of the human child lying helpless in his burrow. After such a long winded explanation they all ask, "Can you help us Mr. Benjamin for time is running out and we must get her back to the human world as soon as possible?"

"Yes! Oh! Yes! I will leave straight away," answered Mr. Benjamin Wedge Tail Eagle and off he flew.

It was a short flight over the mountains for Mr. Benjamin with his huge wings. He reached the caves in no time but needed to distract the huge purple dragon on guard at the entrance to the dark caves. Huge flames poured from the purple dragon's mouth when he spotted Mr. Benjamin.

"Oh!" cried Mr. Benjamin, "where are the Fairies when you need them?"

Just then down flew a band of Pixies with little bombs filled with water from the sparkling river nearby. One by one they bombarded the purple dragon creating a distraction so Mr. Benjamin could sneak past into the caves and find the yellow dew drop flowers. They were only tiny so he had to look hard to find them. A turn here and a turn there through the caves he went and finally, on the edge of the open entrance to the other end of the cave, he found the tiny yellow dew drops growing. He delicately picked one up and placed it gently in his beak. Mr. Benjamin wondered how the pixies were getting along but he couldn't stop to thank them as he was in a hurry.

"I know I will return later and thank them for their efforts," thought Mr. Benjamin to himself as he flew out of the opposite entrance to the caves and back to Mr. Pickles burrow.

The nurses carefully squeezed several drops from the delicate dew drop flower while Mr. Prickles held Anci up so that they could more easily give her the right dose. "Yes!" said Mr. Pickles, "I believe she will be all right now. We must return her to her own world immediately."

So Mr. Benjamin took her clothes in his beak and with little Puttsy holding tight to his legs he flew them home and left them near granny Appleseed's beautiful garden beds.

Due to the lateness of the hour Granny Appleseed was beginning to panic when Anci and Puttsy had not returned. "Oh! Dear! Where can they be?" said granny in an agitated state. I must go and look for them. She wandered out the back door and down towards the garden beds.

"Oh!" she cried when she saw Anci lying there near her beautiful garden beds. Shaking her gently she began to cry, "Oh! Anci. My poor little Anci. What! Oh! What has happened to you?"

Puttsy was barking and carrying on as if he was trying to tell her. Granny looked down at Anci and saw the big lump on Anci's forehead. Picking Anci up to carry her inside granny said to herself, "I must call Doctor MagPai. He must come immediately."

In a short space of time Dr. MagPai arrived just as Anci was coming round.

"Well, granny," said the doctor, "I don't think that you have much to worry about. It looks like she may have a slight concussion from having hit her head when she fell this afternoon. A good rest in bed for a few days will do the trick."

"Granny," cried Anci, "Oh! I fell down a hole and the beautiful pumpkin twin fairies with their lovely pale pink gossamer wings took me to their fairy pumpkin festival and…"

Patting Anci on the head doctor MagPai said to granny, "She must have hit her head hard. It is only her imagination playing tricks don't worry too much. She will be fine in a day or two."

Anci insisted that she did meet the pumpkin twins. "Yes, yes my dear Anci we'll talk more later but for now you heard doctor MagPai rest is what you need," replied granny.

Granny Appleseed was just happy to have both of them home safely.

The Treeless Mountains of Panning Creek

"In Australia, Panning Creek," Philip began, "is 45 kilometres from the nearest town in one direction and a good 20 kilometres as the crow flies in the other. We'll camp there for tonight but before making camp," he said, "I'll take you to a special place I stumbled on while prospecting for gold." He turned the car on to a small dirt track drove over some steep hills, past the old road and on to a farmer's property.

There it was in the middle of nowhere! Three miles of wonderful softwood scrub! Everything else in the area was dead because of the drought but here was a mini oasis!

Huge trees reached up through the sky and enormous boulders were arranged in semicircles. Growing through the centre was a fig tree that had flung its great branches so high it was impossible to see the top. It was watered by a natural spring seeping up through the ground and was incredibly beautiful!

I climbed up and along the rocks and sitting down saw a Spiny Ant Eater huddled against them. There was suddenly small life everywhere. Birds filled the trees while small lizards crawled among the peat on the ground.

Night had fallen quickly at Panning Creek and while we set up camp Philip explained, "There's many who won't camp here in these parts any more. Not since Jenny's untimely death." He became lost in his thoughts for a few moments. "It's the early hours of the morn when the good folks around here claim to have seen her. Jenny, I mean. She's a small figure with long blonde hair and dressed in long flowing robes. Her death was tragic. Her husband and children moved away. But folks say that Jenny still lives here as they have seen her ghostly apparition."

"Jenny is an early riser and stands gazing out across the mountains watching the sun rise in anticipation of a bright new day. Folks have seen her gathering paper bark. Then she is gone, only to return in the wee hours." He continued. "Do you realize," he said, "that you are sitting outside Jenny's old humpy?" He sprang to his feet, "Come on I'll show you round."

The doors were warped and creaked when opened but shut with a loud bang when a gust of wind caught them. The fireplace, table and chairs, a kitchen cupboard equipped with tea, coffee, salt and biscuits and two beds were still in place as Jenny had left them on her death years before. Looking around I could see that most of the humpy was still intact.

As we walked through the kitchen at the front, the torn wire mesh that had once kept out the flies and mosquitoes was in bad need of repair.

We stepped over the split-level concrete into what used to be the bedrooms then walked through a small hallway off which was the fernery and shower room. The back was open and a large 44 gallon drum placed there to stop the moos from wandering through. Out there stood the water tank on its solid wooden frame seemingly on guard like a silent, lonely sentinel and because it was almost empty made a strange tinkling sound leaving you with an eerie feeling.

In daylight the house was easier to explore. "It wasn't always like this. Jenny had her a fine market garden, fence and all, that's the only way one could stop the moos from eating everything. Fertilized naturally of course with manure from the bum nut layers," he said.

The guided tour now over, we placed our gold pans in the car and set out for Philip's old claims.

As we drove I couldn't help noticing that all the mountains looked the same. "Absolutely treeless!." Philip explained that when he first came to Panning Creek to pan for gold years before, these mountains were covered in a thick dense forest and softwood scrub the same as he had shown me earlier. "Back then," he went on, "you needed a compass to get around these parts or you'd become lost for sure."

What then had happened to this forest in such a short time?

He began to explain that a combination of the drought and farmers were the major cause of it. "The drought our farmers have suffered out here of late has left them short of food." My puzzled expression brought a smile to his face as he further explained, "these farmers deal strictly in cattle and cattle eat acres of grass out at a time. There was no rain coming so they needed to help elevate the cattle's food shortage. So this particular farmer chose to poison all the trees to elevate the problem." These mountains once covered in thick softwood scrub were stripped naked by the devastation.

It was terrible!

There were acres of dead trees, some of which were still standing while others had fallen to the ground.

Seeing the anguish in my querying eyes, at the massive destruction that one farmer had caused he said, "He justified it by saying it was necessary to feed the moos. You see with the trees as thick as they were, they stopped the grass from growing and it was grass the moos needed."

The afternoon sun had begun to set and shadows fell on the grass-covered treeless mountains. Former experience had taught him the light fades quickly on a winter's day here at Panning Creek so as a cool breeze had sprung up on arriving back at camp we gathered wood for the fire and prepared the evening meal.

As we sat talking by the fire he explained, "If you hear any loud noises during the night it'll only be the moos. Moos are inquisitive creatures and they'll just be coming to have a look at you," with this he doused the fire and bade me goodnight.

I rose and made my way to my tent and stood there a while to gaze at the brilliant stars that were shinning vividly from the Milky Way.

In the wee hours of the morning I was awoken. The moos were walking lightly around the tent mooing softly. After a short while their little commotion was over and they wandered off.

By this time Philip had arisen and we both stood there in amazement watching the bright fluorescent glow that was radiating from within Jenny's humpy.

The tinkling sound of the water tank sent a repeated eerie chill down my spine.

There she was standing with her hand raised as if to cover her eyes from the coming rays of the rising sun at the same time casting her eyes over the treeless mountains, shaking her head as if in despair. Then stretching her arm in an arc over the mountains as if trying to explain what was upsetting her.

The Trees! Her Trees! That beautiful softwood scrub had gone forever!

Wally Wombat Meets Percy Platypus

Grandma North lived on a farm in the leafy forest mountains. Everyday she liked to walk beside the river that runs down the mountain as it meandered along through the flourishing forest floor. She was looking for anything unusual that she could write about in her journals and one day came upon something extraordinary.

As she walked along the river bank an animal almost the size of a house cat came out of the water in front of her. On land it shuffled like a lizard around the river bank looking for a soft place to make a burrow.

It appeared on the outside to have a slightly oily waterproof brown fur coat and underneath a softer hair that was yellowish in colour. This animal also had a soft blue gray rubbery duck like bill and strong webbed feet with a twelve centimetre long flat tail that it used as a rudder for steering in the water similar to a beaver.

It had grooves in the side of its head for ears that seemed to be sensitive to the sounds around. It had small beady eyes which were receptive to any movement. It had four legs which extended horizontally from its body allowing it to shuffle about on land. Its web feet helped to propel it through the water. While on land the web folded back revealing a sharp claw that was used for digging. This creature stopped not far from Grandma North and she estimated it to be at least forty five centimetres long and possibly weighing up to two kilograms.

It uncovered its claw and began digging its burrow in the side of the river bank which, when finished, was approximately twenty five metres in length. The female mammal from the monotreme family used its burrow to rest in during the day and to lay her eggs. Can you guess who or what it was? Oh! Well done! Of course it's a Platypus.

Not far away from the platypus' burrow another animal was looking for a place to make her warren.

Grandma North feared the worst as these animals are very territorial. So what happens if both animals' burrows intrude on each others? These animals are nocturnal herbivores and also prefer covered hills, mountainous terrain and wet forest areas. This common animal is smart and has a large brain. It can run at 40 kilometres an hour. Their food is fibrous and they can survive without water. They can also drop their body temperature in order to conserve their energy. It is the males who do all the hard work and make the warrens. They dig their burrows out approximately 20 to 30 metres long. They often lay on their sides to dig out the roof and the sides of the warren. It is the females who have it easy and lay their eggs in the males freshly dug burrow. These nocturnal Herbivores clean themselves by laying on their sides and scooping sand over themselves. They cam swim well and have a thick soft fur and can weigh up to 36 kilograms. Native grasses, leaves and roots are their favourite diet and are often very shy creatures.

In the evening before they venture out looking for food they leave their scats outside the burrow so they can find their way home. Scat is the name given to their droppings and all scat droppings smell different. These amazing marsupials are very strong and determined creatures and are known for tunneling under fences. There are three distinct species. The common Wombat, The Northern Hairy Nosed Wombat and The Southern Hairy Nosed Wombat, although one is rapidly becoming extinct. Can you tell me which species it was? Yes! Correct! It was a Common Wombat. Wombats can grow up to 1.3 metres in length and have a large naked snout covered in grainy skin. The common wombats are stout and sturdy and have a large, blunt head with small eyes and ears and a short muscular neck. They cut their food with sharp chisel like teeth which grow continuously.

Grandma North sat and watched as each animal dug out each end of what would become the same burrow. What would each of them do when they came face to face with each other? Would they fight and hurt each other? No! Of course not! Do you know why? Wombats are social creatures and don't mind sharing their warrens with others. Within minutes Wally wombat was face to face with Percy platypus. Wally stopped digging when he thought he heard a puppy growling at him Platypus can make sounds that compare to a puppy growling. Wally began gnashing his teeth while swinging his head from side to side and growling. Wally was tired and this just seemed to be a waste of energy. In the end they greeted each other calmly and went for a swim in the cool water. "How cool is this", Wally said to Percy? "I can walk from my warren right through your burrow to the water instead of having to go around." So after a good swim and a good night's feeding they both shook hands and vowed to always share their burrows with each other on a yearly basis and to become life time friends forever. As the rain began falling they settled down side by side in their own burrows hoping to get a good day's sleep.

Glossary of Australian Slang terms

Anci	*Is a Hungarian name meaning Hannah.*
Alice Springs	*Is a town in the centre of the Northern Territory.*
As the crow flies	*To go directly in a straight line.*
Billy's on	*Boiling water to make tea or coffee usually using a tin placed over a camp fire.*
Billabong:	*Aboriginal name for a trapped body of water.*
Darwin	*Is the capital of the Northern Territory.*
Kookaburra	*A large brown and white bird that feed on snakes and worms.*
A Leprechaun	*Is an Irish myth. It is said that this little man has a pot of gold stashed at the end of a rainbow.*
Simpson Dessert	*Is a desert that lies between the centre of the Northern Territory and South Australia.*
Spiny Ant Eater	*Is a small creature with large quills on its back. It lives on ants.*
Rumbalar	*Is a town in the Northern Territory.*
Brolga	*Is a bird of flight which has a long beak and long legs.*
Butcherbird	*Is smaller than a Magpie but is similar They are a. smaller bird and have black and white colours and have a wonderful song.*
Bum nut:layers	*chicken egg*
Cockatoo	*A large white noisy bird with a yellow crest.*
Crow	*A large black bird similar to an English Raven.*
Australian Crow	*Is small with white tips on their wings*
Dingo	*Australia's native wild dog.*
Emu	*A large flightless bird that can run very fast.*
Galah	*A large grey and pink bird similar to a cockatoo..*
Hare	*Similar to a rabbit with longer ears.*
Humpy:	*Aboriginal name for a house.*
Ibis	*A large bird that flies and digs for worms and other insects in the ground.*
Joe Blake:	*Australian slang for snake.*

Kangahopper:	*Australian slang for Kangaroo.*
Milky Way	*Stars that form in bands across the winter night sky in Australia.*
Moos:	*Australian slang for cows.*
Owl	*A large bird that sleeps in the day and hunts at night. It also eats field mice.*
Red Tailed Parrots	*Are large black parrots with red feathers underneath their tails. Farmers believe that they can predict rain.*
Quails	*Small birds that build their nests in long grasses They can fly.*
Scrub Turkey	*They lay their eggs in mounds of leaves and other vegetation. They are also a protected species.*

About the Author

Betty May Winter writes under the pen name of Elizabeth May Winters. She was born in Brisbane, Queensland, Australia on the 29th October 1949. Her maiden name was Lyddy before she married in 1971. She moved to Rockhampton in Central Queensland in 1975. In 1997 she majored in Drama and Communications at the Central Queensland University. In 2000 she moved with her family to a 110 acre Duboisia property in Tingoora which is in the South Burnett Area of Queensland. Tingoora is an Aboriginal name meaning 'Place of Wattle Trees'. She regularly visits Wooroolin, Wondai, Murgon, and Kingaroy. These are also Aboriginal names. Wooroolin means 'Place of Water', Wondai is the "Place of the Wild Dingoes', Murgon the "Place of Water Lilies' and Kingaroy is the "Red Ant'. The wild animals that she writes about come from these areas. Her first book 'FairyLand' was published in 2007.